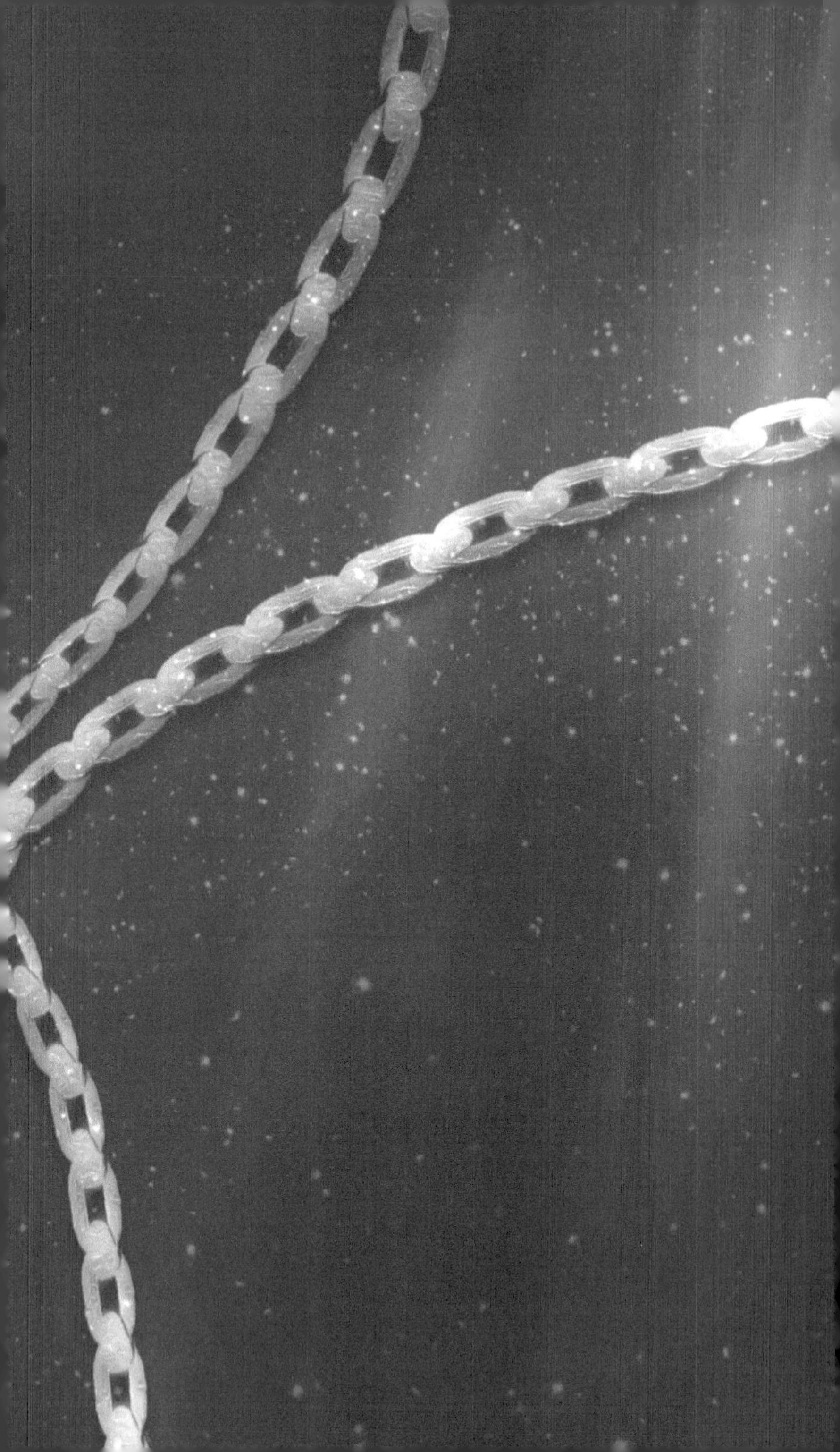

POSSESSIVE

SPARROW AND THE MAFIA KINGS

BOOK 1

MAGGIE ALABASTER

TRIGGER WARNINGS

Hi lovely reader. This book contains darker themes.

Assault
  Abuse
  Violence
  Mentions of sexual assault
  Mentions of child death

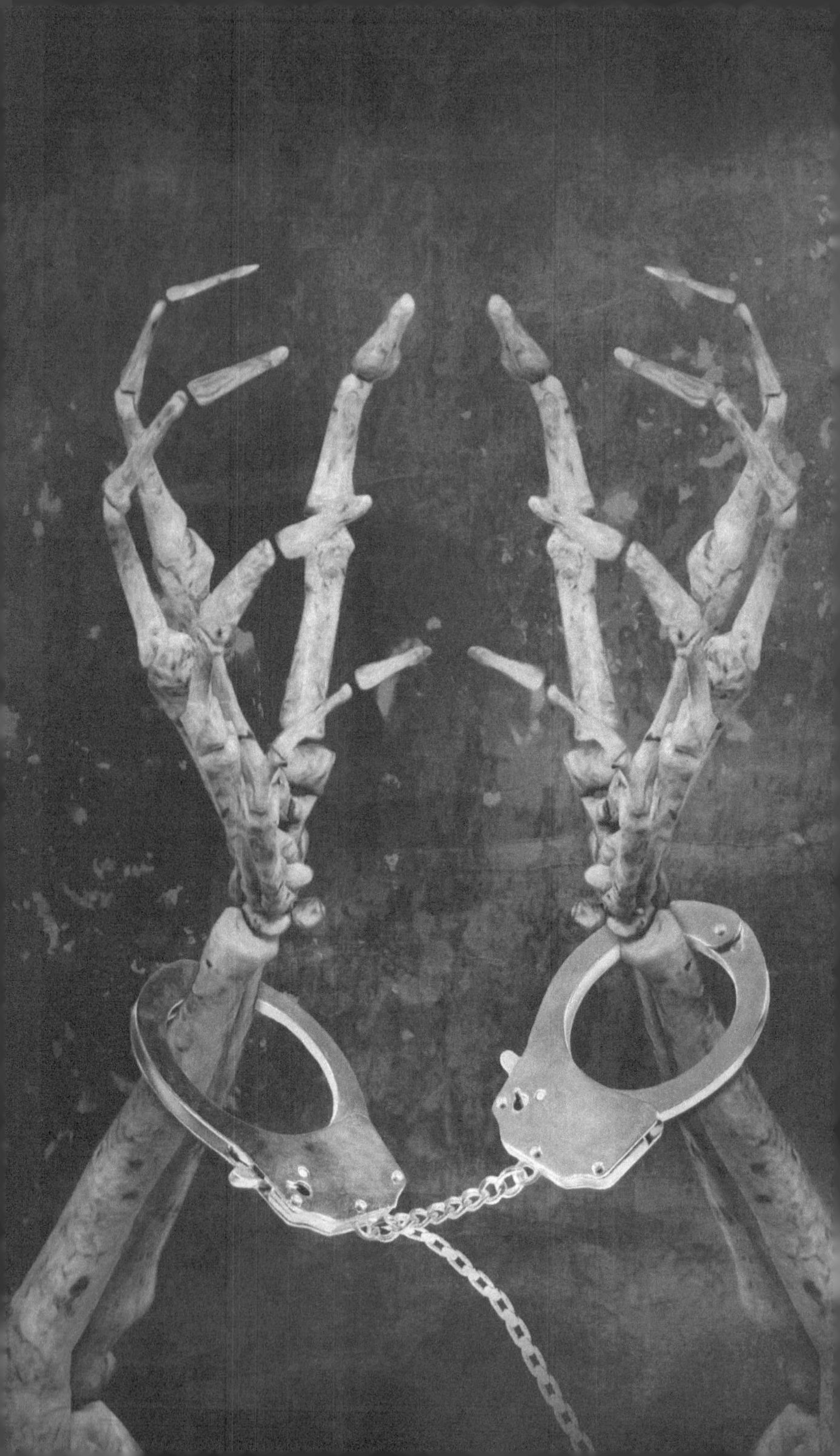

CHAPTER 1

MINA

I snapped awake. Froze, eyes half open in the gloom.

Shoving ragged, matted hair off my face, I pushed myself to an uncomfortable hunch. The rusty bars above me stopped me from sitting fully upright.

I pulled my legs closer to my body. The movement rattled the chain attached to the bars. Accustomed as I was to the strap chafing my ankle, I barely winced.

My attention wasn't on myself. It was on the barely visible outline of the door.

Every muscle in my body tensed, waiting. A minute past, then several more. Each punctuated by the dripping of water down the damp walls.

Just as I started to decide I'd heard nothing, and it might be safe to doze again, the door slowly opened.

"Miss me, bitch?" Kurt Lasalle strode into the dank basement. He crossed his arms and smiled, as though I should be grateful for his presence. Like he owned the place.

Owned *me*.

I didn't answer. Instead I focused on a patch of concrete floor in front of his feet.

Could it please open up and swallow him? If it couldn't, I wished it would do that to me.

The floor remained stubbornly solid.

He kicked the side of the cage, making it rattle and shake. "I said, did you miss me, bitch?"

I flinched and swallowed hard. Of course I didn't miss him. Every moment he was absent was a blessing. If there were blessings in a place like this.

Before I could answer, he dropped a slice of bread through the bars at the top of the cage. It landed near my knee.

My stomach pinched at the sight of it. How long was it since I'd eaten anything? The last time he was here at least. Two days, maybe three.

Not long enough, but too long at the same time.

"Eat it," he barked.

Before he could change his mind and take the bread back, I snatched it up and stuffed the whole piece into my mouth. I struggled to chew. With any luck, I'd choke on it.

Kurt laughed. "You look like a fucking animal."

Bit by bit, I swallowed down the stale bread. Parts of it tasted mouldy, but I couldn't bring myself to care. Focusing on chewing kept me from looking at Kurt.

Of course I looked like an animal. He treated me like one. He chained me in here, naked and filthy. He kept me on the verge of starving. My only source of water, most of the time, was the moisture that trickled down the walls and into the cage.

How long was it since I last saw sunlight?

I barely remembered how it looked, how it felt when it caressed my face. Maybe I dreamt that I used to walk in it, to skip around the garden with my sister and brothers.

Sometimes, when I dozed, I dreamt of that life.

Then I woke to this one. Hour after hour. Day after day. How long had it been? I had no idea. No way to tell night from day. All I knew was monotony, broken by dozing and visits from *him*.

I couldn't sleep here, not properly. Not deeply. I didn't dare. Sleeping was for another life, one that was such a faded memory I wasn't sure if it was real either.

I swallowed down the last of the bread and huddled up against the side of the cage.

Kurt started to pace back and forth in front of it, putting me further on edge. Somehow, he knew what it did to me. That him moving around like he was caged put me further on edge. That was exactly why he did it. He got off on the power trip. On feeling like he had the upper hand on someone. Even if that someone was chained and caged.

"You should be grateful," he said, as though lost in thought about something specific. "After what you did, you should have had your throat cut. You know that, don't you?"

He stopped and crouched down in front of me. *"Don't you?"*

"Yes," I said. My throat was so dry, my voice was a hoarse whisper. The sound was strange to my ears.

I hadn't had reason to talk much for so long. I only did it answer his questions when he insisted on it. Usually 'yes' or 'no' was enough to satisfy him. He wasn't here for a conversation with me, he was here to remind himself he held the power.

Something must have happened to make him need an extra ego boost. I didn't give a shit what, only that I'd bear the brunt of it. I always did.

"Yes," Kurt echoed. "But here you are. Still alive. Because of me. Because I decided to have mercy on you."

I met his eyes for half a heartbeat before dropping my gaze again. His idea of mercy was fucked up. More than fucked up. He'd dreamt up a nightmare and I was living it.

"You're grateful to me, aren't you Mina? Because I was kind enough to let you live. Look at me." He gripped the bars of the cage and shook it. *"Look at me, bitch."*

I raised my gaze again and looked into his hateful face.

If he wanted gratitude, he should drive a knife through my heart. As I was dying, I'd thank him for it.

But not for this. Not for this version of living. I wanted to spit at him, but my mouth was too dry. I resorted to looking back at him with cold eyes, expressionless.

His dark hair was cut close to his scalp. His stubble was as long as his hair. Brown eyes regarded me with amusement. I wanted nothing more in this world than to watch the light fade out of those eyes. For him to die slowly, painfully.

I didn't realise I'd curled my hands into fists until he looked down at them.

"You have some fight in you today, hmmm?" He raised an eyebrow.

No.

No. No. No.

He pulled a key out of his pocket and pushed it into the lock. He swung the door open and grabbed the end of the chain. He stood, dragging the chain with him.

I bit back a whimper of pain. The strap dug into my ankle as he pulled me across the floor of the cage on my ass.

The chain wrapped around one hand, he grabbed my wrist with the other and pulled me to my feet. He shoved me a handful of steps over to a basin on the side of the room.

"Wash yourself," he growled.

I grabbed hold of the side of the sink and held on to keep from falling. My legs could barely hold my weight. The chain was extended to the full extent of its length. I knew from past experience, it wasn't long enough for me to reach the door. Just the cage and the sink.

Before I could even pick up a washcloth, he grabbed the back of my hair, shoved my face under the tap and turned on the frigid water.

I struggled to breathe, but I managed to swallow a few gulps. It was fresher than what trickled down the walls. Not by much. It tasted like it passed through rusty pipes.

He pulled me back out of the water and laughed. "Refreshing enough for you? I should put in the plug, fill the sink and hold you under, but I won't. Not today." He sounded as though he was doing me a favour by letting me live.

He'd do me one if he carried out his threat and let me die. I wouldn't fight him.

He let my hair go and took a step back. "Hurry up."

I didn't want to obey him, but he gave me very few chances to get clean. I felt as though a layer of dirt coated every centimetre of my skin. If I could wash some of it away for now, it would stop being itchy and hard. For a while.

I grabbed the washcloth and wiped my face, before starting to wipe down my filthy body. I would have given almost anything for hot water and a proper shower or bath.

He snatched the washcloth from my hand and scrubbed it hard over my ass and pussy.

"That'll do." He turned off the water and tossed the

cloth into the sink. From a hook on the wall, he pulled a towel and quickly ran it over me. The thin cloth was rough. Abrasive like a cheese grater on tender skin. It couldn't have been much cleaner than I was. Kurt had dried me with it several times already without taking it to wash it. It smelled sharp and musty.

Whatever the original colour was, was anyone's guess. It could have been blue, grey or maybe brown. Hell, it could have been bright pink for all I knew. Either way, it was old and worn. The kind people use on animals, rather than wasting the good, soft towels.

He stepped over to hang the towel back up on the hook. For those few seconds, he had no hand on me, or on the chain.

I stepped back towards the cage. If I was quick enough, I could scurry back inside.

He leaned over, grabbed a section of chain and pulled it, almost tripping me over.

I grabbed the outside of the cage to keep from falling on my face.

"Where do you think you're going, bitch?" He sounded amused. "You really are feisty today." He grabbed the back of my neck and pushed me forward until I was bent over the top of the cage. The cold metal dug into my chest and stomach, rough with wear and rust.

I pressed myself into it as though somehow I could slip between the bars and back into the cage. Hell was better than what he was about to do to me. What he'd done so many times before. I used to fight back, but I'd learnt the futility of that. The more I fought, the better he liked it.

I squeezed my eyes shut and hoped like hell he'd finish quickly.

The sound of a phone ringing echoed through the basement. It sounded so loud, I flinched. After spending hour upon hour in near silence, noises like that were a shock to my senses.

The ringtone wailed with the words to some rock song, the vocals sung by a woman, as far as I could tell.

"My love was a dark place,

Betrayed, denied, and broken.

I was shattered,

Over and gone.

Over and gone.

So gone."

"Fuck," Kurt growled.

He pulled his phone out of his pocket and pressed it to his ear. "What?" he snarled. He listened for a few moments before swearing again. "I'm on my way."

He shoved his phone back into his pocket and yanked me back upright. "Fun will have to wait until later." He pushed me back into the cage and slammed the door shut before pulling the key back out of the lock. "Try not to miss me too much." He smirked.

I'd miss him like I'd miss a bullet in my brain.

I scrambled back into the corner and curled up as small as I could. The cage was so filthy, I might as well have not washed myself at all. I couldn't avoid touching it, but I touched as little of it as I could.

I watched through slitted eyes as he hurried out the door and locked it behind him. It was a reprieve for now, but Kurt Lasalle was a man of his word. If he said he'd come back to finish what he started, then he would.

Tears were useless. Instead I let myself slip into my numb place, where I stopped thinking and feeling too much. I don't know how many times I'd been grateful to my training for allowing me to switch off like this. If it wasn't for that, I would have broken a long, long time ago.

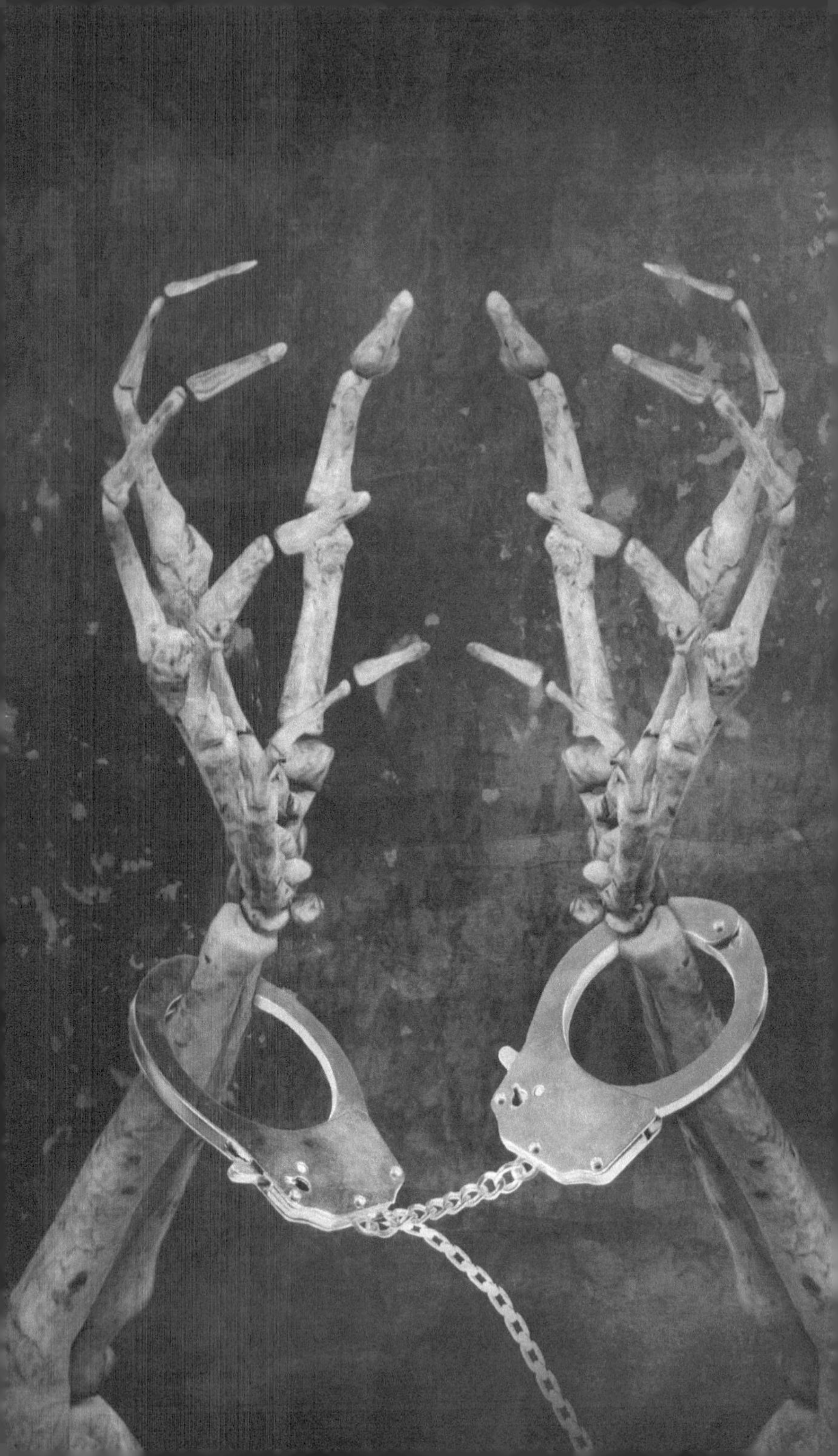

CHAPTER 2

MINA

I huddled with one eye open, watching the door while I let myself drift off again.

The doze wasn't deep enough to dream, not this time. Sometimes that was a mercy. The nightmares left me wanting to scratch my own skin off.

But the dreams were the worst. They helped me escape this hell, but when I woke here, I shattered all over again. Each time felt like a cruel joke. One my brain played on me over and over.

I couldn't blame my subconscious for wanting to take me out of here. It was trying to help me. I wished it would stop. All of it. The dreams, the nightmare and the reality.

Sounds from outside the room brought me fully awake.

Voices. Crashes and scraping from above my head. If

I thought hard enough, I could remember being brought into the building and down some stairs. Upstairs was vague, a hazy memory seen through sedated eyes.

The murmur of voices filtered through the ceiling right above me. I couldn't make out a word they said. Didn't try very hard. I'd heard voices up there before. They never came down here. The one time I shouted, trying to be heard…

I shuddered at the memory. Squeezed my arms tighter around myself.

Heavy footsteps walked across the upstairs floor. Most likely Kurt or someone who worked with him, or for him.

I lay down on my side and try to get comfortable. There was no comfort here, just worse positions than others. I'd grown accustomed to that a long time ago. Deserved it. Maybe more than I deserved to have my throat cut.

What was the saying about the good dying young? I didn't deserve the peace, even though I craved it, more than anything.

The footsteps moved across the floor, down to the end of the upstairs. Slowly, deliberately they drew closer.

I pushed myself up to my elbows and stared at the door.

If I could raise the chain and wrap it round my

throat, I would have. They say it's impossible to strangle yourself, but I would have tried. Anything to stop Kurt from touching me.

Whether or not I deserved everything he did to me, I hated it more than I hated myself. Hated him.

I squeezed my eyes shut and forced myself back into my numb, emotionless place. I had to lock myself in here. I couldn't let him get behind these walls anymore. He always found a way, but I had to keep him out. I had to cling to the last piece of sanity I had.

I asked myself why. Would it be better if I broke? If I lost myself completely. Maybe then I could switch off. Disappear to a place I'd never feel another thing again. Not death, but close enough.

The door rattled.

I frowned. Kurt would have unlocked it. Unless I'd finally lost my mind, whoever it was, they didn't have a key.

The murmur of voices was louder now, just on the other side of the door. Two distinct voices, at least.

"In my experience, people who keep things behind locked doors have something to hide," one of the voices said.

The others said something that sounded like agreement. "Open it."

A handful of moments later, something slammed against the door.

It held.

"Feels solid to me, boss," the first voice said. "Can I shoot the lock off?"

Apparently he was allowed to, because the question was followed by a gunshot, so loud it hurt my ears.

I clapped my hands over them and shrunk down, wincing.

The door swung open slowly.

"Ugh, it stinks in there, boss." In the gloom, I made out a figure waving a hand in front of his nose.

"You've smelled worse, Gianni," his boss said. He pulled out a phone and turned on the torch.

"True, boss," Gianni agreed. "I've probably *made* worse smells."

His boss grunted and stepped into the room, moving his phone around to illuminate the space.

I half closed my eyes against the sudden glare. They hadn't been subjected to light that bright in too long.

Gianni pulled out his own phone and waved the torch around the other side of the room. He stepped off to the side and stopped in front of the cage. He shone the light right at me. "Um, boss?"

I threw my arm up in front of my face to shield my eyes.

"What—" The second man turned. "Fuck."

"Fuck is right," Gianni said. "Is that…"

One of the men crouched down in front of the cage, not close enough to touch it with his expensive suit.

"Yes, I believe it is." He turned his face into Gianni's light.

My breath caught in my throat. I knew that face. Those cold, calculating ice blue eyes that saw everything. The strong chin covered in a layer of stubble. The strong mouth, often set in a line of disapproval.

He turned back to me, his voice a combination of gravel and honey. He never raised his voice. He didn't have to. When he spoke, people listened, before leaping to do what he said.

"Mina DiMarco, what are you doing here?"

"Reuben," I whispered.

He turned to Gianni and nodded.

I'd never believed in a higher power. No one was coming to save me from this hell. Not until now. Finally, I could get the one thing I craved so much.

Finally, I could die.

I ducked my head and waited.

"Get her out of there," Reuben said.

"On it, boss." Gianni nodded. "You might want to cover your faces." He slid out his gun and aimed it at the lock on the cage.

Reuben rose and stepped aside.

Elbows down to cover my chest, I put my hands over my eyes and tried not to wince at the second gunshot. The bullet slammed into the lock, blasting it into splinters. The cage door creaked ajar.

Gianni forced it open all the way, the hinges squeaking in protest.

Reuben slid off his suit jacket and offered it to me,

along with his hand. The first I accepted and wrapped around myself. The other, I just stared at.

"I can't—" I tilted my head toward the strap around my ankle.

"I'm starting to hate this Lasalle prick," Gianni remarked. He put away his gun and pulled out a knife. "I'm sorry, sweetheart, this is going to hurt like a bitch."

He climbed into the cage and gripped my calf with surprisingly gentle fingers.

I flinched at his touch, but not enough to dislodge his hand. I didn't have the strength for that, even if I wanted to. I hated myself for my weakness, but I hated Kurt more.

Gianni and I had that much in common.

"How the…" He grunted.

"What is it?" Reuben asked.

Gianni directed the answer at me. "How long has this been on here? It looks like the skin has tried to grow up around it." His dark eyes looked angry, but not with me. There was a coldness about him, but a softness as well. The contract was too conflicting for me to figure out right now.

Reuben swore under his breath.

I could only shrug slightly and shake my head. "I don't know." I drew Reuben's jacket around myself tighter as Gianni searched for a place to slip the knife and cut the strap.

"Can you hold the light over here, boss?" He nodded towards my ankle.

Reuben stepped closer, holding his torch over Gianni's hands.

"It's lucky I like sharp knives." Gianni glanced at me and grinned before slicing through the leather of the strap like he was cutting an overcooked steak.

"This might suck." He put his knife away and gripped the two sides of the strap. Slowly and carefully he eased it away from my ankle. The leather stuck to my skin and the flesh underneath it.

He was right, it hurt like a bitch. The skin stung, trying to hold onto the strap like it was a part of itself. Every so often, he had to stop and push the skin down to pry the leather off.

"This has to have been there for… If I had to guess, I'd say years." He worked it loose and finally tossed it aside.

I blinked away tears of pain and forced myself to focus on what was more important. I was no longer attached to the chain. I could hardly grasp what that even meant. Was I free after so long, or was this a whole new level of hell?

I guessed Kurt hadn't invited them here. Otherwise they wouldn't have needed to force their way in, or break the lock in the cage. Unless this was some kind of sick game.

"Come on, sweetheart." Gianni backed out of the cage.

After a brief hesitation, I followed, crawling out and grabbing the side of the cage to pull myself to my feet.

"What the hell did he do to you?" Reuben asked softly.

"Where is he?" I peered towards the door. He said he'd come back. If he did, he'd find us all here.

"My guess is he saw us coming and ran," Gianni said. He seemed cheerful at the idea. Like he was amused at Kurt's cowardice.

"We'll deal with him," Reuben said darkly.

"Slowly and painfully," Gianni said. "If you want, you can watch."

I glanced at him. If anyone was doing anything slow and painful to Kurt, I wanted to do more than watch.

"We have some talking to do," Reuben said. He nodded towards the stairs. "Can you walk?"

I seemed to have three options: stay here, be carried or walk. I wasn't doing the first. The idea of either of them touching me gave rise to a spike of panic.

"I can walk," I said finally. "What are you going to…"

Reuben Brantley was high up in a huge organised crime network here in Australia. The Australian mafia, if you wanted to call it that. Before Kurt, our families were at odds. I couldn't rule out his intention to kill me, or worse.

"We're going to get you out of here." It was Gianni who replied. "Right, boss?"

I heard him referring to Reuben as boss several times now. Of course things would have changed since I was here, but the changes seemed to be bigger than I would have expected. I filed that thought away for later.

Reuben glanced at Gianni and stepped out of the room and up the stairs, leaving us to follow.

"I won't let anything happen to you," Gianni said. He made no effort to lower his voice. He wanted Reuben to hear what he was saying, whether he agreed with him or not.

Reuben grunted in response.

I grabbed hold of the handrail and strained to pull myself up the first couple of steps. I knew I was weak, emaciated. Until now, I hadn't realised how badly. I hadn't walked more than a few steps in…

"How long?" I asked softly.

Reuben stopped at the landing and turned around. "According to your father, you ran off to marry some nice boy and live in the suburbs."

Of course that was the line my father concocted. He would have had to tell people something.

"How long?" I asked again.

He pressed his lips together for a moment. "Five years. That was five years ago." He turned back around and continued up the stairs.

I put a hand over my mouth. If Gianni hadn't grabbed me, I would have fallen back down the stairs. Could it be possible? And yet, I knew it was. It felt like a lifetime and it almost had been.

I lowered my hand. "I was eighteen."

"Then you're owed a few birthday presents," Gianni

said. "Five of them. You must be twenty-three. I really, really hate Kurt Lasalle right now."

My head was spinning so fast I had to let him help me the rest of the way up the steps.

I'd missed out on five years of my life. What else had I missed out on?

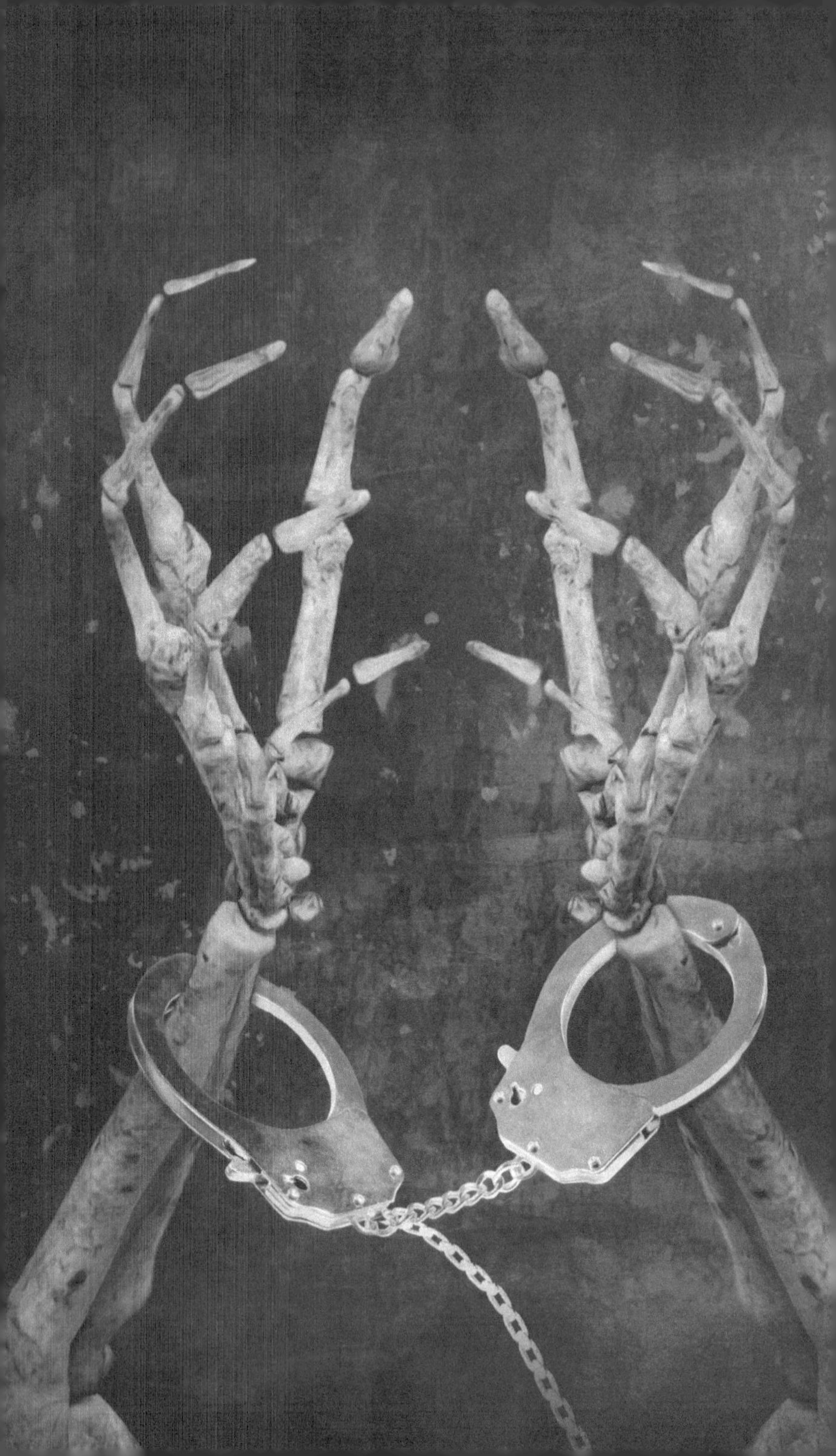

CHAPTER 3

MINA

Gianni lowered his hands from me when we reached the top of the stairs. He stayed close while we moved through the house, his whole body on alert.

Upstairs was a different world from the basement. Hardwood floors and expensive-looking furniture. Art on the walls. Hooks for them, anyway. Several paintings lay on the floor as if they'd been pulled down and left in a hurry.

Reuben's doing, I presumed. What was he looking for here? Not me. That was obvious from the shock when he first saw me. Had they found what they'd come here for?

The answer became evident when another man met us at the door. He was taller than Reuben and Gianni, with lighter hair and a tighter expression.

"Nothing, boss," he said briskly. "If Lasalle was doing what we were told he was doing, he's not doing it from here." His gaze slid to me. His eyebrows knitted and his mouth drew back.

Reuben nodded. "We'll find something in the other locations. I want everyone to keep looking." He stepped out the front door, toward a dark coloured sedan which was parked at the curb. "And Damon, tell them I want Kurt Lasalle alive."

"On it, boss." Damon took out his phone and sent off a quick text before making his way to the driver's seat.

I stopped at the threshold and recoiled from the glare. From the look of the light, it was late afternoon, but it was a brighter light than I'd seen in years. With the exception of the torches on their phones. Those were brief, this was overwhelming.

I wiped tears from my eyes.

"Boss," Gianni called out.

Reuben opened the passenger door and reached inside. When he stepped back towards the house, he held out his hand to me.

I had to blink a couple of times to realise he held pair of sunglasses.

I took them, opened the arms and slid them onto my face. They were much too big for me, but they filtered the worst of the sunlight.

"Thank you." That was something I hadn't said in a long time. Something I hadn't had a reason to say.

"We've spent enough time here," was Reuben's inpatient reply before he returned to the car and slipped inside.

That was an understatement.

I followed Gianni to the car and climbed inside, grateful for the tinted windows, comfortable seat and carpet under my bare feet. This felt like luxury after the cramped, filthy cage.

Gianni got in on the other side and sat far enough away to give me space, but close enough that I couldn't ignore his presence.

I felt like an injured bird he'd found on the side of the road and put into a cardboard box to nurse back to life. Just like me and my brother Asher did when we were kids. Our eldest brother, Dane, always told us we were wasting our time, but sometimes the animals lived. Usually with the help of our sister, Rose. She always seemed to know the right things to do.

"I'd ask if you're okay, but we both know the answer," Gianni said, his voice low to keep the conversation between him and me. "You will be."

The look I gave him should have conveyed my scepticism. How can I possibly, ever be okay? Did I deserve to be?

I clicked my seatbelt and curled my legs up on the seat beside me. I carefully arranged the jacket to cover as much of me as possible. For a piece of fabric, it felt like armour between me and the world. Like somehow I could hide behind it. It wasn't about modesty so much as it was about having a wall around me, however flimsy.

Damon glanced over his shoulder, frowned briefly, but put the car in drive and headed into the city traffic.

Pressed down as low as I could get, I watched flashes of the city go past. Nothing I recognised. Either everything had changed, or I wasn't familiar with the area to start with.

Whatever it was, I could have been on an alien planet. Other cars, other people, nothing felt real. Life had gone on without me. People had continued to live theirs while mine was on pause.

"You must be wondering how we came to be in that house today, of all days," Gianni said.

I turned back to him. I had wondered that. If I was honest, I wondered why they weren't there sooner. Maybe they were and never had cause to look in the basement.

"So, Kurt Lasalle works for Reuben," Gianni went on. "In theory. Obviously he didn't have permission to keep a girl in his basement. If we knew that, we would have gotten you out of there ages ago."

It hadn't occurred to me they might have known I was there and just left me there. It should have. Men like these, they had no loyalty to someone like me. Just to themselves and to each other. Even then, loyalty wasn't assured. Everyone has their price, as my father used to say.

"Lately he's been getting into things he shouldn't be," Gianni added. "Overstepping his authority. We've heard from a reliable source that he's been operating a few side hustles on his own. And not paying his dues. Reuben doesn't like it when people do that."

That was a lot to unpack. First of all, reliable sources were hard to find in their line of work. Secondly, was the suggestion Reuben was in charge now.

"What about Reuben's father?" I asked.

"Dead," Gianni said simply. "Both of his parents. But that's a story for him to tell." He nodded toward Reuben, who'd turned his head, indicating he was listening.

Of course they were. The Brantley family had their share of enemies five years ago. It didn't surprise me someone took them out. It sounded as though there was more to it, but I didn't ask. Not now.

"So you came after Kurt?" I asked. "Thinking he was hiding something back there."

That would explain the paintings on the floor, and them breaking into the basement.

"He's definitely hiding something," Gianni said. "Apart from you, of course. Although, now we know about you, fuck knows how many other girls out there he has locked away."

That thought made the single piece of bread in my stomach threaten to come back up.

Of course at some point in the last five years, I'd wondered if I was the only one, but he never gave any indication there might be others. That didn't mean there weren't.

"We'll be searching all of his properties," Reuben

said. "Thoroughly. And all of his contacts. Whatever he's hiding, we'll find it."

"I want to help," I said.

Reuben swivelled around in his seat to fix his ice blue eyes on me. "I'll consider it. When you're well enough."

Eighteen-year-old Mina might have argued with him, telling him she was perfectly capable of both helping and looking after herself.

The Mina of the present day, who could barely support her own body weight, just nodded slightly. There was little I could do apart from answer the questions if they asked any. Which they would. If it helped them to pin down Kurt, I'd tell them everything I knew. I was painfully aware that wasn't very much.

I leaned against the door beside me and closed my eyes. I didn't dare to doze here, but maybe someday I'd feel safe enough to sleep. Really sleep.

When I opened my eyes again, Gianni was watching me. He might give someone else the creeps with his intense stare, but he had an air about him. If I could trust anyone in this world, I could trust him.

Letting myself trust, that was another story. I was the little, broken bird in the cardboard box. Desperately wanting to fly, but needing to lie there under the old towel and gather my strength. Listening to kind words and careful gestures, but barely able to grasp that they could possibly apply to me.

I turned my gaze back outside the window.

"This must all seem strange to you," Gianni said. "It all seems strange to me too, and I haven't been through what you have."

I looked back at him, brow furrowed in question.

"You're wondering why I find it strange?" he guessed. "I suppose it's just that all of these people, living so close together, seems to me like a weird thing to do. People in general, I find their weirdness fascinating. I want to know why they do the things they do. Damon likes to tell me someday my curiosity will get me killed."

"It will," Damon said over his shoulder.

Gianni grinned. "See? But if there's any trouble, Damon is always the first to leap into it. Who do you think will get killed before whom?"

"Still you," Damon said. "I'm always careful."

Gianni cupped his hands around his mouth and whispered loudly. "No he's not. If he was careful, he'd stay home and knit."

Reuben snorted.

"Fucking *knit*," Damon muttered. "I don't know how to knit and neither do you."

Gianni chuckled. "It's so easy to get him going." He lowered his hands to his thighs.

"And that's why you'll get killed first," Damon said. "You'll piss off the wrong person and they'll shoot you."

"Are you threatening me?" Gianni looked completely unworried.

"Yes," Damon said. "Yes, I am. Can I shoot him, boss?"

"No," Reuben said simply. "Not today. Focus on what Lasalle is up to. Damon, have you spoken to his sister?"

"Ohhh, I wouldn't want to be Kurt when Daze finds out what he did to Mina," Gianni said. "We'll be lucky if she leaves his big toe behind for us to find."

When I looked questioningly again, he said, "Daisy Lasalle also works for Reuben, she's a bit of a badass, and she hates when men do bad things to women. When she learns about you, she's going to tear him a new one, brother or not. You're going to love her."

His description made me curious to meet her. Whether or not I'd love her remained to be seen. Was I capable of loving anyone? I wasn't sure but I was certain of one thing—it was impossible for anyone to love me. How could they after what I did?

Did they know about that? I supposed not, unless they left me alive so I could keep eating myself up with guilt.

"Not yet," Damon said, as if Gianni hadn't spoken. "You want me to go and see her, boss?"

"No," Reuben said. "Have her come to us. If she's working with her brother, I want to see it on her face. If she's complicit, she's dead."

"You think Daisy Lasalle is working behind your back?" Gianni asked.

"No, but blind trust gets people killed," Reuben said.

He turned back to look at me. The message was clear. They'd been speaking very openly in front of me, but he wasn't sure if he could trust me to keep my mouth shut.

I looked back at him. Who would I tell? If he thought for a moment I was working with Kurt, he was out of his fucking mind. There was no one left for me to confide in.

Kurt had thoroughly enjoyed telling me when my parents and siblings died. He'd laughed while I sank further into despair. For a while, I thought one of them might come for me. When the last of them was gone, my hope went with it. I never expected to be found and freed by a Brantley. Especially not Reuben.

No, they could speak as openly as they wanted to. I wouldn't say a word to anyone.

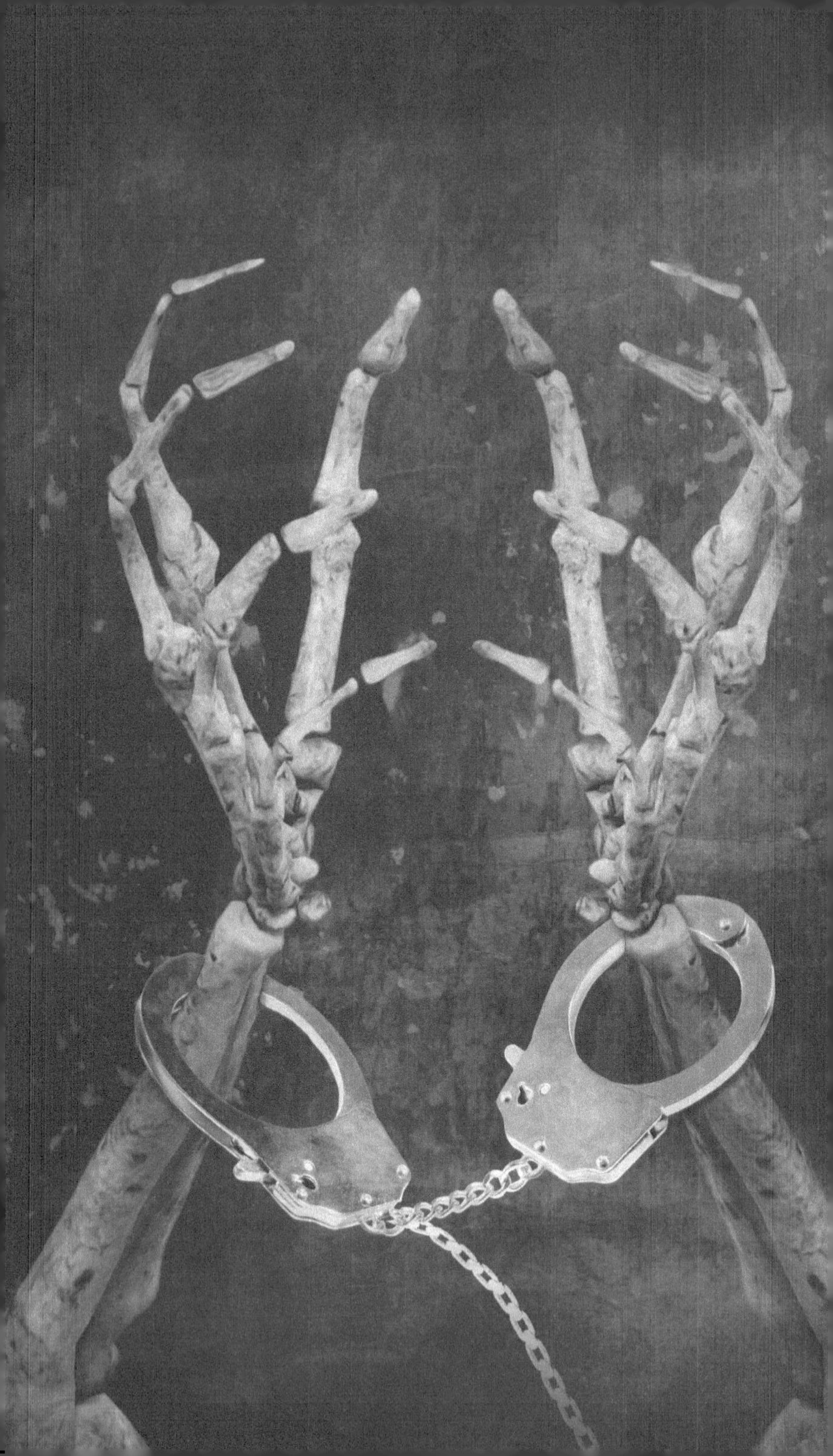

CHAPTER 4

MINA

Damon pulled the car into the garage of a large, but otherwise unassuming, brick house. A high, stone fence and a patch of land surrounded it, keeping the suburb around it at bay.

Reuben climbed out of the car and over to the interior door. "Gianni, take care of Mina." He disappeared inside, followed by Damon.

"You heard the boss," Gianni said. He waited until the garage door closed behind us, leaving us in dim light.

I undid my seatbelt and pushed open the door. Swallowed hard. I pulled the sunglasses off my face and held them in trembling fingers.

This isn't the basement, I told myself. *It's just a garage.* But I wanted to shrink back into the car and curl up on the seat. Let it be my cardboard box.

"It's okay," Gianni said softly. "I've got you. I'm going

to snip off Lasalle's toes, one by one, when I catch up to him, but I've got you. Come on, step away from the car."

"I don't know if I can," I said. The walk to the door felt too far, too long. Too exposed.

"I can carry you," Gianni offered.

"No," I said quickly. I recoiled from the idea, and from him.

"It's okay if you want to stay here for a while," he said. "But there's a bath inside. Or a shower, if you prefer. And food. Terry made pizza last night, I bet there's some left over."

"Terry?" I asked in a quavering voice. I hated the sound of it. I was Mina DiMarco, I was stronger than this. I'd survived everything Kurt put me through. I wasn't going to break down now.

"He's Reuben's butler and chef and whatever the hell else," Gianni said. "He looks like a mountain, but he's harmless."

"The opposite of you," I said without thinking.

Gianni chuckled. "Something like that. I'm nice on the outside, but Reuben keeps me around because I know a variety of ways to get information from people."

"Torture?" I asked.

"If it comes to that," he agreed. "It's not my preferred method, necessarily. I don't hurt people for the fun of it, unless they deserve it. So, bath or shower?"

"With hot water?" I asked.

"As hot as you want," he agreed. "Unless you prefer cold?"

"I never want to feel cold water again," I said. I managed to push the car door closed behind me, but I leaned against the outside of the vehicle. Partly for physical support and partly for emotional.

How fucked up was I that a strange car felt like a safe place?

It was the first place in five years I could sit up and see daylight. The first surface I'd sat on that was actually comfortable. It was so small, but so big at the same time.

"Then you don't have to," Gianni said. He moved around in front of me and offered me his hand. "I understand being touched might be terrible. Just think of me as a crutch. Lean on me until you can lie down in the bath and get clean. Don't think of me as a person, if that helps."

I stared at his hand. "Why are you being so nice to me?"

The question made him frown. "Sweetheart, we found you in a cage, chained up like a wild animal. Don't you think it's time someone was nice to you? Also, Reuben told me to. But I would have anyway. You remind me of myself."

That statement made me blink. "How am I anything like you?"

"Some people think I'm an animal too," he said. "Like I said, I know a variety of ways to get people to talk, including torture. I don't flinch at blood, urine or screams of pain. Does that sound like a normal person to you?"

"In the world I grew up in? Yes," I said. He might be right that we were alike, but I didn't think he really understood how much.

He grinned. "I should have expected that answer. It sounds like your childhood was as fucked up as mine." His smile faded. "More so."

"Yeah." I pushed myself off the side of the car and started to slow walk to the door.

Halfway there, I had to grab his elbow to keep from falling. Through the fabric of his button down shirt, his skin was warm, reminding me he was definitely not just a crutch. He was a living, breathing person, and that was something I should be wary of. Whether or not I thought I could trust him, he was still a man. One who stood over a head taller than me. In my current state, it wouldn't matter what skills I had. I wouldn't be able to fend off him or anyone else.

That forced me to decide. I had to go along with them for now. I had to do everything I could to get fit and strong, until I could defend myself. Besides, the idea of pizza was enticing.

"That was what I thought," Gianni said.

I glanced sideways at him in confusion.

"You're stronger than you think you are," he said. "You're a fighter. I wouldn't expect anything less from a DiMarco."

"We're known for our stubbornness." I followed him inside the house.

He stopped in the middle of the dark hardwood floor. "There's no bathroom down here. I just remembered. Can you manage one more set of stairs?" He looked annoyed at himself.

"I can manage," I said. I let go of his elbow and made my way to the staircase leading upstairs.

It looked as though it had been there for a hundred years, along with the rest of the house. This must have been one of the first in the area, the suburbs growing up around it. The property had probably been in the Brantley family for a handful of generations. And now it belonged to Reuben.

I grabbed hold of the thick banister and pulled myself up step-by-step, while Gianni walked behind me. He made no attempt to touch me, or come too close. He just kept himself near enough that if I needed help, he'd be right there.

"You know mobsters aren't supposed to be nice," I said over my shoulder.

He chuckled. "I like to be different. Although, you're the first person who's ever called me nice. Usually it's something like 'that psychotic prick who works for Reuben.' Obviously they don't know me very well. I'm not psychotic, I'm creative."

I snorted softly. "I see how those two things could get confused." I had some experience in that myself. In another lifetime.

"Go to the right at the top of the stairs," he said.

I did what he said, and stepped into a large bathroom. The floor was covered in black and white penny tiles, and the walls with white subways. In the back corner, was a large shower. Beside that was a freestanding, clawfoot tub. Opposite the bath was a vanity with light timber doors and double sinks, with a marble countertop. Everything had a colonial look, but new, like it was recently remodelled.

"Looks expensive," I remarked.

"Nothing but the best for Reuben," Gianni said. He opened a cabinet that matched the vanity and pulled out a couple of towels. He set them down beside the bath and turned on the water. "Let me guess, you're a lavender kind of girl?"

"I'm a girl who probably smells like a week-old corpse, I don't really care," I said.

"I didn't want to be rude." Gianni winked at me. He pulled out some purple bath salts and sprinkled them into the rising water. "If you climb in, I'll work on your hair."

"You'll—" I stared at him.

"My mother was a hairdresser. If anyone can do anything with it, it's me. Unless you want me to get Damon. He'll just bring a knife and cut it all off." He made a hacking gesture with his hand.

I put a hand to my head. I hadn't given much thought to my hair. Not for a long time. Every so often,

Kurt would hack it shorter, but all I could do was run my fingers through it once in a while.

I stepped over towards the bath and caught sight of myself in the mirror. If I didn't know it was me, I never would have recognised myself. My cheeks were sunken in, my hair was tangled. My eyes looked huge in my face, greenish blue and haunted, surrounded by long lashes. I touched my cheek to make sure it really was me.

"I don't just smell like a week old corpse, I *look* like one," I said.

"Nothing a bath and trim won't fix," Gianni said. "Hop in." He turned his back and waved towards the bath.

He'd already seen me naked, but I appreciated the gesture. Especially given it was brighter in here than it was in the basement. In this light, I'd never hide all the scars.

I slipped off the jacket and stepped into the water. I closed my eyes and groaned at how incredible the warmth felt. I sank in, under the bubbles, and moaned again.

"It sounds like you're enjoying that," Gianni said. He turned around and hurried over to the vanity to pull out shampoo, conditioner and a pair of scissors. He knelt behind me and carefully started to wash my hair.

I flinched when his hands first touched my head.

He was still for a few moments, waiting for me to

tell him to back off or keep going. Eventually, he started to slowly massage my scalp.

I grabbed up a bar of soap from the side of the bath and started to wash off years of dirt and grime from my skin. My ankle stung where the strap had been, as well as several other scratches and scrapes, but none of that detracted from how incredible it felt to be surrounded by hot water. Water that wouldn't stay clean for long.

"I'm going to rinse your hair," Gianni said. "Can you scoot down a bit?"

I slid down far enough to submerge the back of my head while he rubbed off the shampoo. I sat back up so he could apply the conditioner.

Using a wide tooth comb, he started to tease out some of the tangles. Every so often, he stopped to pick up the scissors and cut out a knot.

"He could have at least given you access to a hair-brush," he grumbled.

"If you have to cut it all off—" I started.

"Not all of it," Gianni said. He breathed out a frus-trated sigh through his nose. "More than I'd like. Don't worry, you'll look adorable when I'm done with you."

"I'll settle for clean," I said.

"That, I can guarantee," he said. "There we go. Let's rinse off your hair again."

My head felt several times lighter when I lowered it into the water again. The rinsing took a lot less time.

"There we go. You'll feel like a whole new woman

now." He stood and put everything away before picking up a towel and holding it out to me.

I could have stayed in there for hours, but the water was turning brown, so I stood while he averted his eyes, and took the towel. I wrapped it around myself and stepped out of the bath.

"I'll leave you for a few minutes," he said. "I'll ask Terry if he can find you some clothes." He hurried out the door and closed it behind him.

I pulled off the towel and quickly dried myself. A quick glance in the mirror showed my filthy, matted hair was now gone, replaced by a cute bob. Gianni saved more of it than I expected.

I still looked like a stranger to myself. How long would it take before the woman in the mirror looked like me?

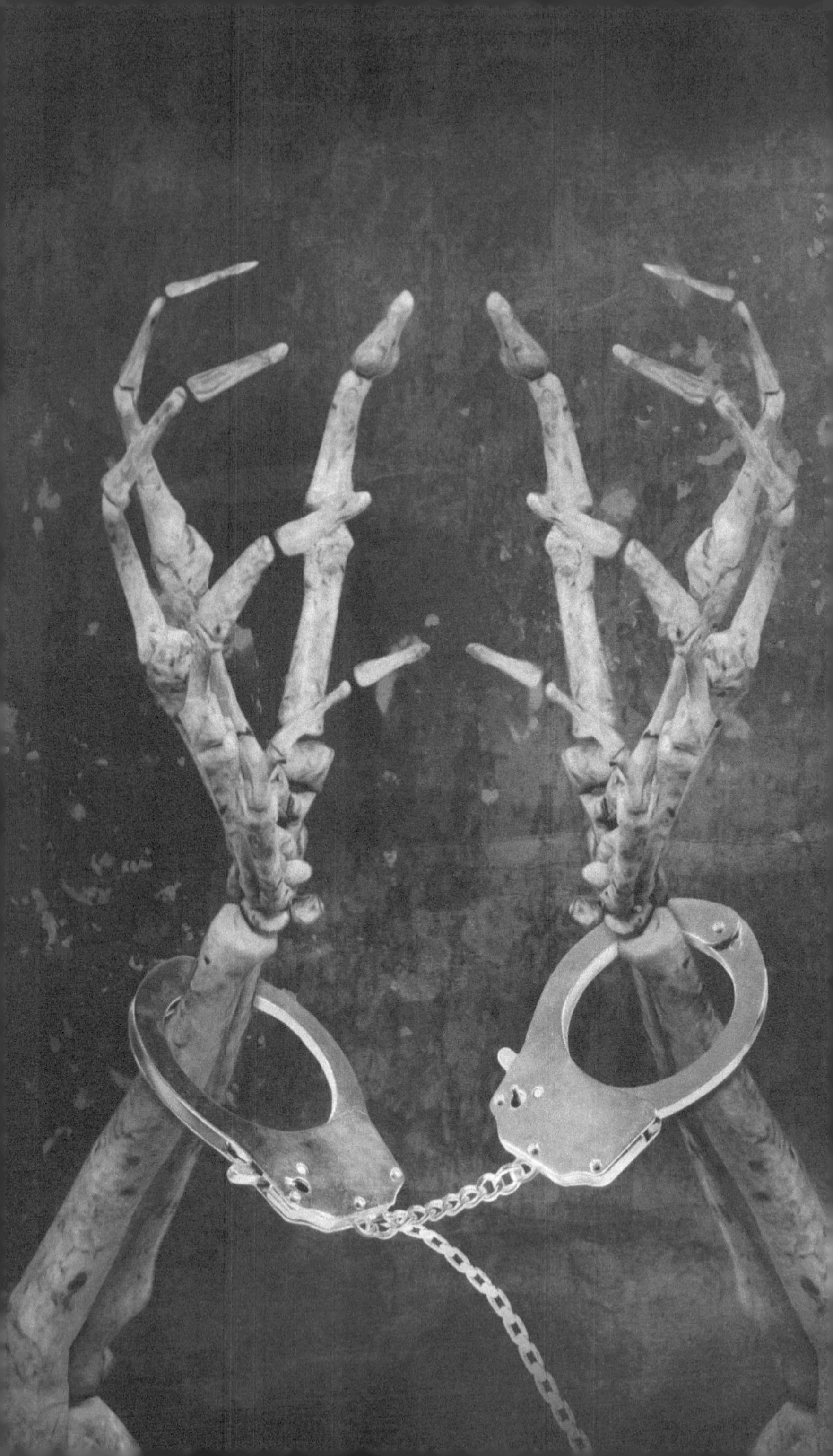

CHAPTER 5

REUBEN

I glanced up from my glass of whiskey as Damon stepped into the room. As always, his expression was guarded, closed. I trusted him more than most, but I gave up trying to read him a long time ago. He got the job done, that was what mattered.

He lowered himself into the leather chair opposite me and sat with his ankle resting on his opposite thigh.

"She wasn't what we were expecting to find," I said.

"No," Damon agreed. "Should we have?"

"I don't know." I scrubbed a hand over my face. "We've kept close track of all the members of the DiMarco family. Not close enough, apparently."

It wasn't guilt I was feeling, but rather irritation at not knowing something I should have known.

Men like Kurt Lasalle shouldn't be able to keep a woman chained up in their basements without my knowledge. Especially one I'd known all her life. What was that ridiculous nickname her family gave her? Mina Sunshine, because she was always happy and smiling. When was the last time she was either of those things?

I struggled to reconcile the girl I once knew, with the woman we found only a handful of hours ago.

"Wild guess the DiMarcos had no idea," Damon remarked. "Not unless there was something in it for them."

"What?" It was a pointless question, he had no more answers than I did.

"Are we going to tell them?" he asked.

"Not yet." I sipped my whiskey, savouring the way it burned down my throat. "I want to talk to her first. She may be able to shed some light on the situation. If any of the DiMarcos knew she was there, they may try to act against us if they learn we have her here."

Damon made an indeterminate sound in the back of his throat. He wasn't scared of them either.

"What are you planning to do with her?"

That was the question I'd had running through my head since I recognised the filthy woman with the big, blue-green eyes. Leaving her there wasn't an option, but I hadn't decided what happened next.

I'd speak to her and make my decision based on that conversation. No doubt Gianni would try to influence me. He was treating her like an abandoned kitten, in need of food and attention to nurse it back to health.

But kittens grew into cats and cats had claws. Especially ones with the last name DiMarco.

"I'll decide that when the time is right." I didn't have to explain myself to him or anyone else. I hadn't had to for a long time. That was how I liked it.

"The boss is probably in his library." Gianni's voice came from just outside the doorway. That was followed by him looking in and smiling. "Here he is."

He stepped into the room. My breath caught in my throat as Mina followed him in.

She'd never been tall, but she was all but swallowed by the grey track pants and T-shirt she wore. Clothes that used to belong to the twins, if I had to guess. Neither Hunter nor Parker fit into them since they were ten or twelve, but they'd remained stashed away in a box somewhere until now.

Even in old, borrowed clothes, she was stunning. Even with the wary, on-edge look in her eyes. No one would blame her for that, least of all me.

"Sit down." Gianni waved towards a chair. "I'll see how Terry is going, heating up some food for you." He actually gave me a warning look before slipping back out the door. He was protective of our little stray. That better not cause a problem.

Damon looked at me questioningly, but I nodded for him to stay.

Mina stepped carefully into the room, looking around the shelves of books that covered the walls.

Some of the shelves weren't filled yet, leaving spaces here and there that I tried to avoid looking at. They looked untidy. If there was anything I hated, it was mess.

She finally slid into a chair and tucked her feet up beside her. She wrapped her arms around herself in a classic, protective pose.

"You're looking better already," I said.

"It's good to be clean." She tucked a few strands of hair behind her ear.

I usually preferred longer hair on women, but it suited her better that way than tangled and matted.

"How did you end up with Kurt Lasalle?" I didn't believe in beating around the bush. I had questions and I wanted answers to them.

"My father gave me to him to settle a debt," she said softly. Did she always speak like that, or was she holding back because she was scared?

"What debt?" I asked.

She shook her head slightly. "I don't know. Just that there was a debt. I guess it didn't help, since my father was killed shortly after that."

"How did you know that?" I asked.

"Kurt told me." A frown furrowed her brow. "He told me when each of my parents and siblings were killed."

I ignored the strangled sound Damon made, and placed my whiskey glass on the table beside me. I leaned towards Mina, my elbows on my thighs.

"He told you your siblings were dead?"

She blinked a couple of times, those long lashes brushing her cheeks. "He said I didn't deserve to know, but he told me anyway."

I sat back. "He told the truth about your parents. Your father had mine killed, so I had them killed. But your siblings are very much alive." I watched as my words slowly sunk in.

She recoiled slightly, but then sat forward again. "Dane, Rose and Asher?"

"All alive," Damon said.

Mina turned towards him. She didn't look like she was sure she should believe a word we'd said.

"Dane teaches history at Brutham Academy," I said. "Rose is down in Melbourne doing whatever Rose does." She was good at solving problems, like disposing of unwanted corpses.

"Asher is..." I sighed. "A drummer in a band with my brother, Zeke." I hadn't given up on the idea of my brother quitting the band to come back to join the family business. One way or another, I'd convince him to stop wasting his time singing rock songs to sold out arenas all over the world.

Mina looked back and forth between us, her pretty mouth slightly open, plush lips quivering.

"It's true." Damon pulled out his phone and tapped on the screen for a minute or two before passing it over to her.

She took it from his hand and looked at the photo on

the screen. Her blonde haired brother stood beside my younger brother, with the rest of the band.

"It says this photo was posted three days ago," she said. "He's really alive." She stared at the photo for the longest time, not moving, barely breathing.

"We can contact them if you like," I offered.

"No." She surprised me with her quick response. "I don't want any of them to see me like this. Not yet. They'd... I can't." She pushed the phone back toward Damon.

"You don't have to," I told her. "You can hide out here for as long as you need to."

Had those words come out of my mouth? Judging by the raised eyebrow, Damon was surprised to hear it as much as I was. We never took in strays. But now she was here, I couldn't bring myself to let her leave. Didn't want her to.

"Thank you," she whispered. "I don't know what to think."

"About what?" Damon asked.

She looked down in the direction of her knees, then back up again slowly. "I thought the reason they didn't come for me was because they were dead. But they weren't. Why would they leave me there? Why would they let him do the things he did to me if they were alive to stop it?" She closed her eyelids over her shining eyes and bit her lip.

"Why didn't they come for me?"

"My guess is they didn't know," I said, my voice

quiet, even for me. "Asher, in particular, would have done anything to get you out of there if he was aware. Rose too."

Dane was a self-serving son of a bitch, who knew what his agenda might be?

"They didn't know," she echoed. "My father must have lied to them too."

"As far as anyone knows, you ran off to marry some nice boy and live in the suburbs," Damon said. "They say you kept in contact for a while before you didn't. They must have thought you were happier away from this life."

"I never contacted them," she said. "I couldn't. Kurt... Kurt had my phone. He must have sent messages, pretending to be me, and they never thought to question it. No one ever thought to try to find me."

"They might have tried," I said. "They wouldn't have been successful. If I had to guess, I'd say the only one who knew about the connection between you and Kurt was your father. Once he was dead, only you and Kurt knew, and he wasn't saying anything."

"And I couldn't." She chewed on her lip. "If you hadn't had my father killed—"

"I doubt he would have told anyone," I said. "I can't imagine your siblings would have taken it well if they knew. If I hadn't had him killed, they would have. Or someone else would have. He was good at making enemies." And giving his innocent daughter to a monster. My only regret was that he didn't die slower.

"He was," she agreed. "I'm glad he's dead. I don't believe in hell, but if it exists, I hope he's there. And I hope Kurt goes there soon."

"He will," I assured her. "I have a lot of resources on finding him. The twins have assured me they are on his trail." Hunter and Parker were both pains in my ass, but they were useful in their own way.

"The twins are… I guess they grew up," she said.

"My youngest brothers got older, but I don't know about growing up," I said dryly. There were twenty years between me and them, so they had time. If they didn't get themselves killed first.

"I feel like I got left behind," she said. "Everything has changed. I don't know where to start to catch up."

"I recommend you start with pizza." Gianni stepped into the room and handed Mina a plate.

Her eyes huge, she started to eat.

"Don't eat too fast," Gianni warned. He crouched down beside her like he might snatch the food away again at any moment.

She moved the plate away from him, as though that might stop him from taking it, and bit into the pizza, a look of bliss on her face. Terry made the best pizza I'd ever had, but it must be just this side of heaven for her.

Watching her eat, the urge to keep her here grew stronger. I wanted to see her experience all of the things she'd missed out on in the last five years. Fresh air, sunshine and good food. Safety, security and stability.

Usually I wouldn't give a shit whether anyone

enjoyed those things or not. But with her, things were different. I was drawn to her. The need to protect her was overwhelming.

Maybe I was getting soft, but I didn't give a fuck. If anyone lay a hand on her, they'd lose it.

I snapped out of my thoughts as she made a gagging sound. She pushed the plate towards Gianni, clapped a hand over her mouth and staggered towards the door.

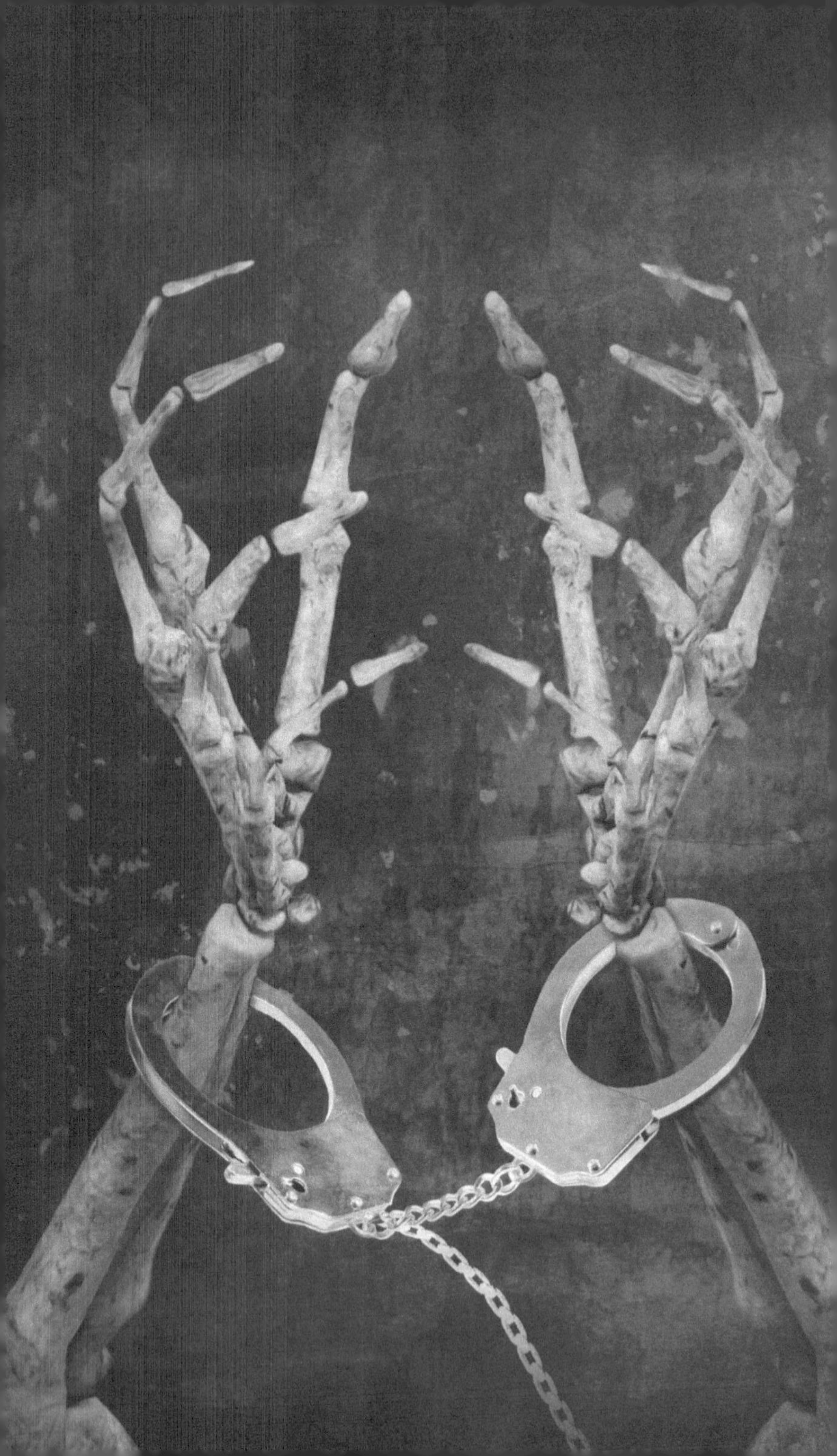

CHAPTER 6

MINA

I lay on my side, my hand on my bloated, sore stomach.

After throwing up the first few mouthfuls of pizza, I kept down some dry crackers and sips of juice. That meagre meal was more than I'd eaten in too long. The taste though…

Even watered down juice tasted like heaven. Clean and fresh and full of flavour. I could easily have ignored the pain and eaten a whole box of the crackers. If I did, I'd throw them back up. My stomach wasn't ready for that much food, even if the rest of me was crying out for it.

I flinched as a shadow stopped in the doorway. Surrendering to a spike of fear and panic, I curled up around my cramping stomach, even as I made out Reuben's silhouette in the light from another room. It illuminated the corridor and most of the room I lay in.

The bed under me was like a cloud after living on

concrete. It was almost too comfortable, the blankets too heavy and warm. I'd pushed them aside and lay straight on the mattress.

"Better?" Reuben stepped inside, arms crossed as though he needed to defend himself from me. He had no reason to be physically intimidated by me, so I wasn't sure what was behind his posture. Something about me had him on his guard. Vice versa was true, so I'd lay no blame on him. Not yet.

Was I better? I wasn't sure. I hadn't thrown up for long, but it was long enough.

"I suppose so," I said. "I shouldn't have eaten so fast." I was lucky to have made it to the powder room in time. Otherwise I would have thrown up all over his hardwood floors.

"I don't blame you." He picked up a chair from the side of the bedroom and placed it down next to me. "For any of it."

I wanted to tell him he should, but I wasn't ready to explain why. The time for that would come when I was feeling stronger. When I was better able to defend myself against him and anyone else.

"I have a doctor on the way to see you," he said. "A discreet one. Anything you have to tell him won't leave these walls. If it does, I'll deal with him."

Of course he would. Someone like Reuben Brantley didn't like his orders being disobeyed.

"Like you dealt with my father," I said.

"Exactly." He sat forward, his elbows resting on his

thighs. "I can't imagine how you survived those years. I'm not sure I would have." That was a surprising admission, coming from someone like him.

"I'm not sure I did," I said. "Maybe I'm dead and I haven't realised it yet."

He responded with a soft snort. "Does that make me the devil? Some would say it does."

"I don't think this is hell," I said. "Unless all those years were Purgatory and I've finally moved on."

"I'm no angel, so I'd suggest you're still alive." He didn't smile when he said that, but his words were slightly lighter.

Now I thought about it, I couldn't remember having ever seen him smile. Maybe that was something he didn't do.

"That's a possibility." I sucked in breath and held it for a long time before slowly letting it go.

"What is it?" he asked. It wasn't quite command, but he gave no apology for prying either.

I pushed myself to sit up against the headboard, my knees tucked into my chest.

"I'm scared of waking up," I whispered.

He took a moment to process that. "In case this is a dream and you're still in the cage."

"Yes." If I woke up and found myself there, the last shred of my sanity would shatter. I was certain of that.

He ran the tip of his finger across his lower lip, back and forth with mesmerising slowness.

"I won't offer to pinch you. I can assure you, this

isn't a dream. Not, I think, a nightmare either. Your fear sounds rational. Expected after what you've been through."

"My mother used to say that people shouldn't make promises they can't keep," I said.

"That's good advice," he said. "I have a preference for operating the same way."

"Then I can believe you if you promise this is real," I said. Could I? I wanted to.

"I promise you, this is real," he said. "You're in my house. I can also promise you that Kurt Lasalle will never touch you again. He will be dealt with appropriately." There was a slight emphasis on the last word. It promised that when they found him, Kurt would suffer.

"I believe you," I said.

"This wasn't what you expected," he stated. "When you first saw me, you thought I'd have you killed. Why?"

I chewed my lip. "I believed Kurt when he said my family was all dead. He suggested you had them killed. I thought I was the last of us. Why wouldn't you have had me killed?"

Reuben inclined his head slowly. "Now you know that's not the case. I've had no reason to go after any of your family, after your father. Not your brothers, your sister or even your cousins." A brief frown creased his brow.

"What is it?" I asked. I hardly knew my cousins, but

when he mentioned them he seemed troubled somehow.

"Gianni mentioned Kurt's sister Daisy," Reuben said. "One of her boyfriends is your cousin, Ric."

"Gianni said Daisy would have Kurt killed if she knew what he did to me," I said. "You think Ric knew?"

Reuben grunted. "No. He wouldn't have kept something like that from her. She'd rip his balls off and make him eat them."

I was starting to like her. She sounded like one hell of a woman. "You think there might be conflict between them because her brother did this to his cousin?"

"Conflict is bad for business," Reuben said. "If it becomes a problem, I'll deal with it. I assume you don't want your cousin knowing you're here either."

I unravelled myself a little, to relieve the pressure in my stomach. Eating would get easier, but it would take time. I'd have to be gentle with myself until then.

"No I don't," I said. "I don't want him to see me like this either." It was probably irrational to feel ashamed about the things Kurt did to me. No one said the human brain was completely logical.

"No one blames you for what he did," Reuben said.

"I do," I said. "I wonder if I could have fought harder. If I did something different, he would have let me out of there. Or maybe he would have stopped coming."

Reuben leaned forward a couple of centimetres, not

close enough to touch, but looking like he wanted to. "You would have preferred to die down there alone."

"When I thought you'd kill me, I was relieved," I admitted. "I gave up on living a long time ago. I gave up fighting when he…" I swallowed hard.

"Forced himself on you." Reuben was always blunt, but he was pulling no punches tonight.

"Yes," I whispered. "He liked to toy with me. To see how long it would take before I cried or screamed."

I gripped the hem of my borrowed T-shirt and raised it up, above my stomach. It was too dark in the basement for him to have seen the scars, but from a sharp intake of breath, he saw them now.

He lifted a hand towards me, but stopped a centimetre or two from touching my skin. "What—"

"Cigar," I said simply. He'd sit beside the cage smoking one before pressing the hot tip against the sensitive skin of my stomach. Or my back.

Reuben swore under his breath. "Sadistic prick."

I lifted the T-shirt higher.

"Fucking hell," Reuben growled.

I glanced down at my bare chest. One of my nipples was perfectly normal, slightly erect in the cool air. The other was nothing but an angry, twisted scar. The skin melted around it was a testament to how long he'd held the tip of the cigar in place. He'd laughed while he did it. Laughed harder when I screamed in agony.

I dropped the shirt back down. "That was the first time I wished I was dead."

I thought I might break that night. Hoped I would. That was also the night I stopped fighting. I hoped he'd tire of me and stay away. Or better yet, kill me.

"He's going to wish he'd never been born." Reuben's tone was one I hadn't heard from him before. It sent a chill up and down my spine. If it was directed at me, I would have been terrified. But it wasn't. His fury was *for* me, on my behalf. I didn't know why, but it was.

"This is why I don't want my family to see me," I said softly. "I'm not me anymore. I'm a broken doll."

Ice blue eyes fixed sternly on me. "You are not broken. Nor are you a doll. You're a survivor. What you've been through would have destroyed most people. You have all the scars to prove that. But he didn't destroy you. You will get your strength back and we'll deal with Lasalle. Do you think those scars make you ugly?"

"They do." I turned my face.

"Mina," he said softly, making me turn back to him. "You've always been beautiful. Those scars make you even more beautiful. Every one of them shows how fucking strong you are. You said you stopped fighting. You didn't. You've never stopped fighting. You adjusted. You did what you had to do to walk out of there. I don't think you have any idea how fucking incredible that is."

I opened my mouth to say something, but he raised a finger and placed it right in front of my lips, close but not touching.

"I promise you this. I'm going to do everything I can to make you see how beautiful you really are. You deserve nothing less."

"You don't know—" I started.

"I know," he said firmly. "I know."

I leaned my head back against the headboard. "Why?"

He gave a laugh-grunt from the back of his throat. "I don't fully understand that either. I just know this is going to happen. There's a reason we were the ones who found you. I intend to discover that reason, but in the meantime you should get some rest. The doctor should be here soon. I trust him, but Gianni will be there too. If he crosses any lines…"

"You'll rip his balls off and make him eat them?" I asked.

"Precisely," Reuben agreed. "No one fucks with you and gets away with it. No one."

I believed him, but it was still strange. If you told me a day ago I'd be here, and that Reuben Brantley would say those things to me, I never would have believed it. I would have thought I'd finally lost my mind. Could I rule out the possibility he lost his?

"Thank you," I said softly. "I want to be there when you deal with him."

He nodded. "Of course. I wouldn't leave you out of it unless you asked me to." He pressed his hands to the seat on either side of him and pushed himself to his feet. "How much you're involved is up to you."

"Can I ask you a question?" I asked him before he stepped out of the room.

"You can ask," he said. "I can only say I'll try to respond."

"I haven't seen any women in the house since I got here." Just Gianni, Reuben, Damon and a glimpse of Terry.

"There are none," Reuben said. "None but you."

I nodded and lay back down on my side.

He gave me a long, last look before he strode out of the room.

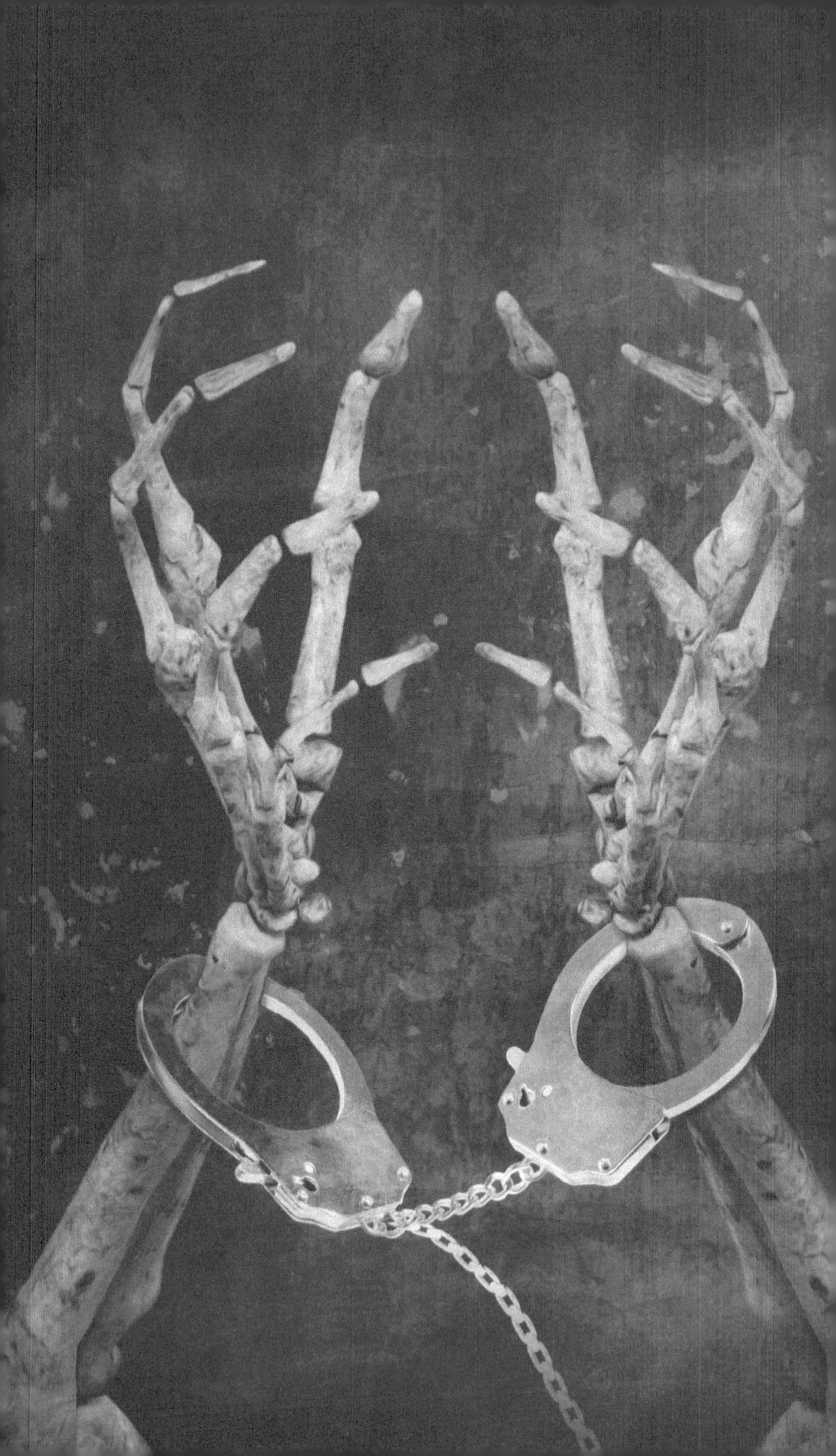

CHAPTER 7

MINA

"Later, Doc." Gianni walked Doctor Ryan out the door before sitting on the side of the bed. "You doing okay?"

"Yeah." I slid under the lightest of the blankets.

The doctor, he'd introduced himself as Oliver, was clearly shocked at what he saw, but he'd been professional. He checked my heart, blood pressure and ankle where the strap dug into the skin. Apart from needing a dose of antibiotics, a tetanus booster, and going easy on food, he said I was in remarkably good health. Physically anyway.

"That's the hard part out of the way," Gianni said. "Now you can focus on the other shit."

"Finding Kurt" I tucked my legs close to my body. "And anyone who worked with him."

"Did you ever see anyone there in the company of that asshole?" Gianni cocked his head at me.

"Saw, no," I said. "I heard them upstairs, but he

never brought anyone down." I remembered a haze of faces from before the basement, but not once I was down there.

"Doesn't mean they didn't know about you," he said thoughtfully, but with a hint of anger. "We'll find them and we'll find out. And have some fun in the process." He rubbed heavily inked hands together.

I shrugged one shoulder. "I just want to find Kurt. Him and anyone else who knew and didn't do anything." I was happy for them to hang beside him.

"In my line of work, I see some shitty things," Gianni said. "This pretty much tops all of that. If there were other people in on what he did to you, that's even more fucked up. We're not known for being nice to each other, but when innocent women are involved, that makes me mad."

I pulled the blankets tight around myself. "Has it ever crossed your mind I might not be innocent?"

He chuckled. "Everyone is innocent if you look at them from the right angle."

"Even you?" I shifted uncomfortably. Between the softness of the bed, wearing clothes and the blanket, everything felt suffocating. I was tempted to throw everything off and sleep on the floor, but I had to regain some kind of normal. To me, that meant sleeping in a bed, with covers over me.

"Asking the big questions, I see," he teased. "In some ways I'm innocent. And by that I mean I'm not always guilty. Damon on the other hand…"

I forced myself to stop fussing and lie still. "What about him? He seems nice enough."

"For a mobster?" Gianni asked with another chuckle. "He's a good guy if he's on your side. If he's not, he's good at fucking people up. The best part, he's good at making people think he's on their side until it's too late." He made a slicing gesture across his throat.

"So I should be careful around him?" I asked. Truthfully, being around so many people was already overwhelming, and it was only three of them. Four if you counted Terry. I'd be more than careful.

Gianni rubbed his chin. "Good question. Damon is dangerous, but no more than Reuben. The difference is, if Damon double crossed you, he'd have me and Reuben to answer to. Does that mean he won't? If he does, he's going to cover his tracks pretty fucking well. There'd have to be a helluva payday in it from someone else, for him if he did that. So yeah, be careful, but don't be afraid to give him your trust either. He's one of the most loyal people I know."

"If he's loyal to you, then you're loyal to him," I said slowly. "What's to stop both of you from turning on me?"

"The fact I'm not an asshole," he said. "I don't hurt women unless I have to."

"Unless Reuben tells you to," I said.

"I've been known to disregard his orders when they go against my moral compass," Gianni said. "Yes, I have one. It mostly points north."

"So you keep turning until it suits you," I said.

He grinned. "Something like that. I've never been the kind of person to follow blindly. Reuben would have to have a very good reason for me to lay a hand on a woman before I'd consider it."

"Like what?" I was getting sleepy, but this was the most interesting conversation I'd had in years, and the least painful. I wasn't ready for it to end yet.

"Like being complicit in handing her daughter to a monster." His expression darkened. "Standing by and letting it happen. Knowing what was going on and saying nothing. Caring more about her own ass than her children."

I pushed the end of the blanket aside with my feet and lay with them sticking out. "You think my mother did that?"

He shrugged. "No way to know now. But if she did, she's the kind of exception I'm happy to deal with."

"How?" I asked. "What could you do that wouldn't make you as bad as Kurt?"

"I don't lay a hand on *innocent* women." He glanced down towards my bare feet.

"Which brings us back to people being innocent." Uncomfortable, I slid my feet back under the covers. "My mother might have been innocent of what you're suggesting. My siblings didn't know, she also might not."

"I hope she didn't." He looked back at my face. "Because that would be a really shitty thing to do."

He was quiet for a moment before jerking up straighter so suddenly I flinched.

"Sorry, sweetheart. It just occurred to me to ask if you wanted to hear some of your brother's music." He pulled his phone out of the back of his trousers. He knelt down beside the bed and tapped the screen to load a video. Holding it sideways, he turned the screen around to face me.

I read the text beside the video. "Wolf… Venom?"

"That's the name of the band. Look, here's where they come on stage."

I squinted at the screen. I recognised Zeke Brantley, who walked to the front of the stage where the microphone was set up. Behind him I caught a glimpse of blonde hair. My heart skipped a beat as my brother slipped behind his drums and picked up his sticks.

The rest of the band took their places. A couple of them looked familiar, but I couldn't put names to faces.

On some cue I couldn't see, they started to play. All of my attention was on Asher, who grinned as he played. He grooved at the same time, looking like he was thoroughly enjoying himself. Of course he did, he'd always enjoyed making music. And life in general. He was the one who should have been nicknamed Sunshine, not me.

"They're not bad, are they?" Gianni asked. "They're one of the biggest bands in the world right now. Living their best life and touring all over the place."

"They're a bit…loud," I said.

They finished playing and Gianni turned off the phone. "That's what Reuben always says too. That they're loud. He prefers his music soft and in the background. If he listens to it at all."

That definitely sounded like Reuben. I couldn't picture him rocking out to music like that.

"What about you?" I asked. "What kind of music do you like?"

"I like it louder than Wolf Venom." He tapped his phone against his knee. "There's a space under the house where we put people when we want to get information from them. It's soundproof. I like to go in there and turn up some metal as loud as it will go. Especially if I'm working with someone in there." He grinned. "When I've had enough of metal, I put on some Carrie Underwood. Or Abbie Hart."

"I've never heard of the second one," I said.

"You're in for a treat." He tapped on his phone again and held it in his palm until a song started.

From the first note, I couldn't contain my reaction. I all but leaped out from under the blanket, threw myself away from the sound and landed on the hard floor with a thump.

"Shit." The song was immediately silent. He jumped up and hurried around the bed to crouch in front of me.

I lay on the floor, pressed hard against the wall, curled up in the smallest ball I could manage. Every millimetre of me was trembling. I couldn't make it stop.

The world was folding in on me, pressing in hard,

making it more and more difficult to breathe. My head was spinning, my stomach turning again. I had to swallow to keep from losing what little I'd eaten.

"I'd understand that reaction to some music, but..." Gianni looked confused and concerned. "If I thought you'd hate it that much, I wouldn't have played it."

He spoke lightly, but he knew as well as I did the song wasn't the problem. That was just the trigger. He was at a loss as to what to say to settle my racing thoughts.

I shook my head, my trembling so bad my teeth were chattering.

"What the hell is going on?" Reuben demanded from the doorway. His footsteps were heavy as he made his way into the room. Commanding attention and making me shrink in further.

"Sorry boss, I freaked her out," Gianni said. "I'm not sure what happened." He looked straight at me, brow furrowed, trying to figure out how to respond to me and to Reuben. That he blamed himself was clear from the expression on his eyes. He was worried he'd fucked up somehow and pushed me over the edge.

I needed to explain, to make them understand. Even if it made me sound like I was losing my mind. Who's to say I wasn't?

I sucked in a couple of rapid breaths, trying to put together the words as simply as I could.

"That song," I whispered. "It's Kurt's ringtone."

The moment I heard it, I was right back in the basement. Chained and scared. Terrified I woke up after all. I couldn't remember what happened after that. I just found myself on the floor, arms wrapped tight around myself, the hard floor a familiar comfort under me.

"Fuck, I had no idea," Gianni said. "I won't play it again. I'll even delete it from my phone." He held up his phone to do just that.

I closed my eyes and struggled back into my numb place. Shutting off everything and everyone around me. I wasn't in the basement, I was here. Safe, warm, clean and fed.

Get a fucking grip, I told myself.

"I'm okay," I said, half to myself. "I'm okay." My hands on the wall behind me, I pushed myself to my feet and sank back down to the bed. "If it's okay, I'd like to be alone now. Please."

"Of course," Reuben said. "We both have rooms just down the corridor. If you need anything." He waved for Gianni to precede him out the door.

Gianni stopped to give me another apologetic look before stepping out.

I slid back under the covers and pulled them up over my head. If I pulled them tight enough, maybe I could shut out the sound of the music that went around and around in my head.

I wasn't sleepy anymore. I was wide awake. With any luck, I might doze a little bit between now and dawn.

Kurt isn't here, I reminded myself. It was just a song.

Just one song out of millions in the world. At least he hadn't chosen one of Asher's songs as his ringtone. That was the kind of fucked up shit he would have done, so he could laugh at the fact I had no idea.

I closed my eyes and willed my heart to stop beating so fast. I should never have freaked out so violently. I needed to be in better control of myself than that. I reminded myself that if I was, I wouldn't have ended up with Kurt in the first place. Somehow, I had to pull myself together, contain myself and keep my emotions and fears from getting the better of me.

I *had* to.

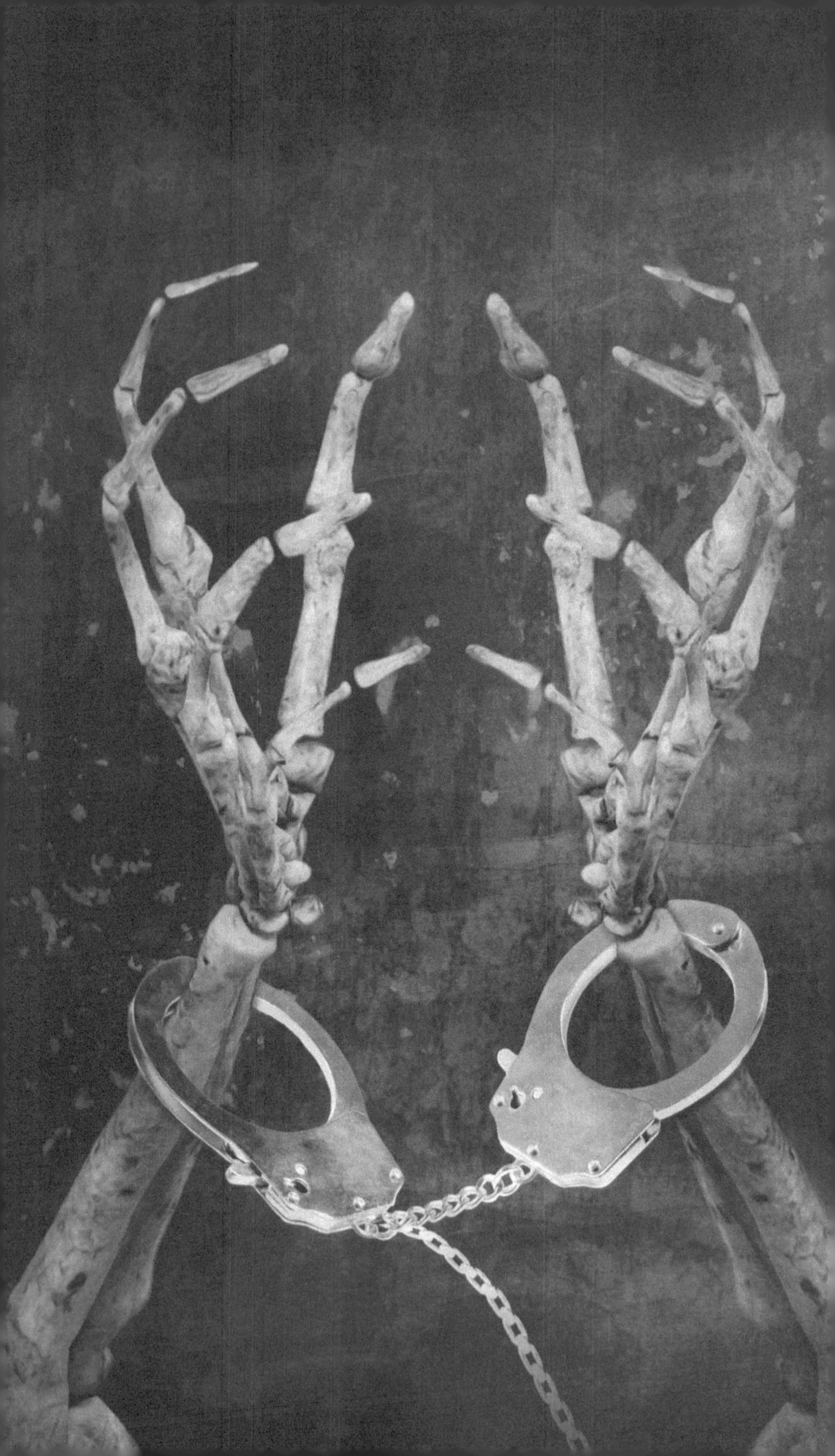

CHAPTER 8

REUBEN

For the last twenty or thirty minutes, I stared at the page without reading a word.

Finally, I slid the bookmark into place and closed the book. If anyone dogeared any of my books, they'd lose a few fingers. As they should. If I was obsessive over anything, it was the condition of my books. Meticulous, clean and with spines unbroken.

I placed the book on the table beside me and scrubbed a hand over my face. At the best of times, I couldn't sleep more than two or three hours a night. With Mina in the house, I was unlikely to get that much.

Gianni once suggested I was at least part vampire. I'd rolled my eyes at him. For his own amusement, he spent the next week with a scarf wrapped around his neck.

I ignored his attempts to goad me, and eventually he stopped wearing it. It might have been Damon's threat to use the scarf to strangle Gianni that did it. Damon was as quiet as I was and just as unpredictable. He may just as easily have carried out his threat on a whim.

Given how irritated I'd be if he killed Gianni, it was best he hadn't.

I suspected Gianni was safe from Damon's hands. They seemed to have some understanding that bordered on a fucked up bromance. Or at least, a mutual agreement not to take each other's lives. I didn't care as long as shit didn't get messy.

I looked up as Gianni slid into the room. Didn't say a word while he sat across from me, his hands steepled and pressed against his lips.

"I scared the shit out of her," he said finally.

"I saw." I heard a rapid shuffling, followed by a thump as she hit the floor.

I hadn't stopped to think, I'd just found myself at her door. Immediately, I wanted to soothe the expression of fear from her face. Fuck, I wanted to pick her up off the floor and wrap my arms around her. If I hadn't thought that wouldn't scare her more, I would have, so I kept my distance.

"I had no idea." Gianni's brow was as furrowed as I'd ever seen it. His dark eyes were troubled. "I showed her a video of her brother and I thought she'd like some other music."

"You couldn't have known," I said. "This won't be the last thing that triggers her."

"I know, I just figured if she could stand looking at

my face, then a bit of music was harmless." His forehead smoothed and he smiled slightly.

I grunted softly. "Apparently there are things in this world more terrifying than your face."

He chuckled. "Reuben Brantley, did you just make a joke?"

My left shoulder rose and fell, barely more than a twitch. "I don't make jokes, just observations."

"I knew you secretly loved me." He laced his fingers together and placed them across his lap.

"So secretly I, myself, wasn't aware of it," I said dryly.

That made him grin more. "Ouch. I have knives gentler than you."

"I'm not supposed to be gentle," I said. "Gentle gets people dead."

He arched an eyebrow at me. "I saw the way you looked at Mina. There's gentleness deep inside you."

I arched mine back at him. "If you ever say that again, you'll be on the other end of one of your knives."

"You know what your problem is?" He tapped his hand against his thigh.

I gave him a flat stare.

As if I hadn't made it clear I didn't want to continue this line of conversation, he went on.

"Your problem is that you think being gentle is a weakness. Sometimes it's a strength. If you softened enough to let someone in, you might find it beneficial."

"I don't need to let anyone in," I said, my teeth gritted.

"Bullshit." He was unflinching. "Everyone needs to let someone in once in a while. Like I said, I saw how you looked at Mina. Like you wanted to tuck her into your pocket and keep her safe from the world. Or better yet, into your pants."

I gripped the arms of my chair and glared at him. "After all she's been through—"

He smiled with something that looked like triumph. "See what I mean? I've never seen you protective of anyone before. Not like this."

I worked my jaw back and forth, but couldn't summon the words to deny the accusation. Finally, I released the arms and placed my hands on my thighs.

"She was a fucking *kid*," I said softly. "What kind of monster hands a kid over to another monster? What debt did DiMarco have that he'd pay for it with an eighteen-year-old girl?"

"Is it because she was eighteen, or because she was Mina?" Gianni asked. "I heard you tell her she was always beautiful." He blinked a couple of times. "Is this why you don't let anyone in? You have a thing for her. For a long time by the sound of it."

"You're stepping very close to dangerous territory," I warned. I usually didn't allow anyone around me to speculate on my personal life, especially not to my face.

Gianni scoffed as only he could. "You're not going to have me killed because I figured out you have a crush. I don't blame you. I have a bit of a crush on her myself. I want to protect her from all the shit in this world. All the bad people who might want to hurt her."

"We are the bad people," I pointed out. "We're exactly the ones she should be protected from."

"Are you going to let her go?" He cocked his head, but he already knew the answer. He was nothing if not intuitive and he knew me better than most people. Sometimes it worried me that I'd let him get too close. Other times, having someone see through my stony façade was a relief.

"No," I said firmly. "She's not…well enough to leave here. Oliver Ryan was adamant about that."

"And when she is?" Gianni pressed. "In a week, or a month, or a year, when she's well enough to walk out the front door, are you going to let her?"

I averted my eyes. "No." It was as simple as that.

"Because?" He shot back. "Because you've already decided she's yours. Now you have her here, you want to keep her here."

"She's mine." I looked back at him, my jaw firmly set. "I'll make sure she knows that."

"And if I want her too?" His jaw was just as firm.

Gianni with his mind made up was insurmountable. He rarely needed to be so rigid, but when he was, nothing, and no one was moving him. Not a single millimetre.

I was just as stubborn, but I could have someone killed if they tried to get in my way.

"That's a conversation for the future," I said. I didn't bother to threaten him. If Mina wanted both of us, I wouldn't deny her. I didn't let myself think about what would happen if she didn't want either of us. She had too much healing to do to contemplate any of these possibilities yet. Healing we'd help her through.

"I'm going to have to find out what kind of music she likes," he mused, the tension leaving the conversation. "She didn't seem to be a fan of Wolf Venom."

"Then she has good taste," I said. My brother's band was not music I enjoyed. Another advantage when he quit and rejoined the family, was that I wouldn't have to hear any more of it.

"She might prefer Blazing Violet or Ice Blue Roses," Gianni mused.

I grimaced. Blazing Violet was at least as loud as Wolf Venom. According to the twins, both bands would be touring together soon. Along with Abbie Hart. She seemed to hold some influence over my brother. I made a note to have the twins bring her to me for a little chat.

"You should try listening to something that was released more recently than twenty years ago," Gianni said.

"I'd rather read books," I said bluntly. "Books aren't loud."

"Audiobooks can be loud," he pointed out.

"Have you ever known me to listen to an audiobook?" I asked.

He rubbed his chin with his thumb and forefinger. "Now I think about it, no I haven't."

"Because I don't," I said.

"Is this one of those 'audiobooks aren't real books' things?" he asked.

"No, it's one of those 'I prefer quiet,' things," I said. I couldn't concentrate on voices reading out loud to me. My mind wandered too much. Maybe if I had fewer thoughts fighting it out in my head to be noticed, I could focus on something like that. Right now, only reading a physical book shut out the noise. For the most part.

"Yeah, I guess you do," he said. "You tend to leave the room when the screaming starts." He wasn't accusing, just stating a fact. When the people he was slicing into started to shriek, I made myself scarce.

"I have better things to do than listen to you torture people." He was right though, I did leave the room before the noise became too much. One of the benefits to being the boss was that I didn't have to subject myself to things I didn't want to be subjected to. That included ear piercing sounds that gave me a headache.

"You don't know what you're missing." He rubbed the palms of his hands together and grinned.

"I know exactly what I'm missing," I said dryly. "Which isn't relevant. I pay you to do things like that so I don't have to." Just like I paid Terry to cook and the twins to do various odd jobs, and Damon to keep them in line.

"That's what I love about this job," Gianni mused. "I get paid to have fun."

"Maybe I shouldn't pay you," I said. "You might turn up and do it for free."

"If you didn't pay me, I'd have to go and work for the Bell family," he said. "I hear Samuel Bell has a—"

"I don't give a shit what Samuel Bell has," I said.

I wouldn't stop paying Gianni, because he might do just that. And if he did, I'd have to have him dealt with. He was too good an asset to let go like that. I wouldn't admit it to myself, but I was accustomed to having him around. He was good at what he did, including taking care of Mina. Scaring the shit out of her with a song, notwithstanding.

"Not even if it's bigger than yours?" Gianni teased.

I rolled my eyes. "Nothing he has is bigger than anything of mine."

The Brantley and Bell families had been rivals for as long as anyone could remember. So long, I wasn't sure anyone knew how it started. It didn't matter, it wasn't ending anytime soon, unless one of our families was wiped out.

Gianni chuckled. "That's what I like about you, boss. You don't pull any punches. You know who you are and you don't give a shit what anyone thinks about you."

That wasn't true, I cared what Mina thought. She was the only one since she got old enough for me to really look at her. I'd wanted her back then, but her father got in the way. If I had any clue what he'd done, I would have prevented it, no matter what it took to do that. I would have paid back his debt and taken her for myself. Her life and mine would have been very different.

Now she was back with me, it was time to put us back on that path. As far as I was concerned, it was inevitable. No matter what I had to do to convince her of that.

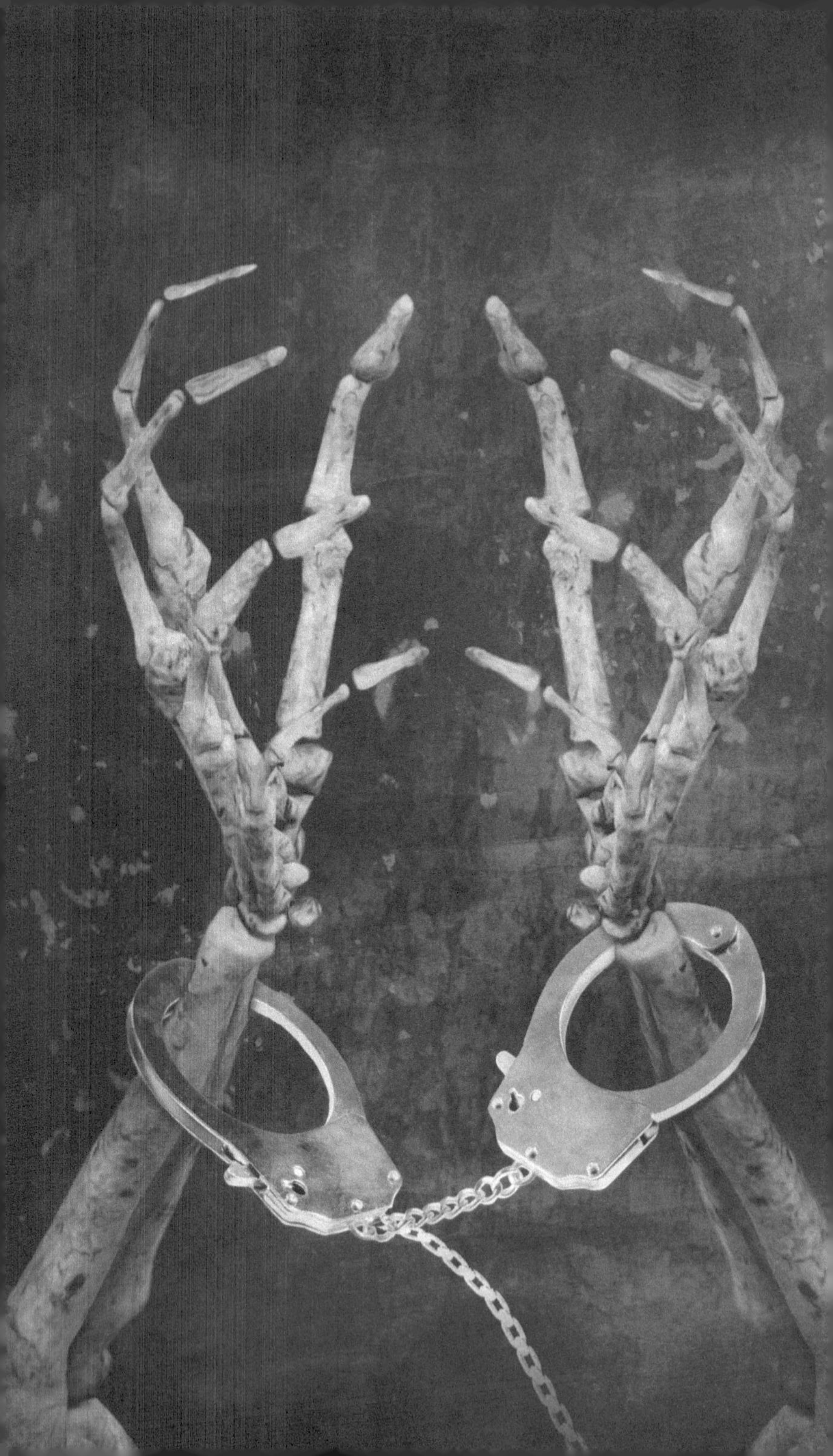

CHAPTER 9

MINA

I managed to get some sleep before dawn. When I awoke again, the house was in near silence. Someone, I guessed it was Terry, was in the kitchen. Every so often dishes rattled, or a pan or pot.

I pushed the tangle of blankets off myself and slipped downstairs and into the library.

Ever since I could remember, I found the company of books easier than that of other people. My mother used to say, you could tell a lot about a person by their books. I was intrigued by what books lined Reuben's shelves.

I wasn't surprised to find a section of classics, but many looked untouched. One or two were still housed in shrinkwrap. Another section contained non-fiction, mostly history.

The biggest sections were fantasy and adventure. All of the books were in good condition, but *Lord of the*

Rings looked slightly more loved than the others. I wasn't sure what I expected, but it wasn't that. Maybe a worn copy of *Sixty-Nine Shades of Morally Grey*.

I flinched as someone walked past the door. Their footsteps stopped a metre or two past before they turned back and peered into the library.

"Hey." He stepped into the room, his hands pressed into his pockets.

It took me a few moments to recognise him. "Hunter? Or Parker?"

He grinned. "You were right the first time. Parker is bringing in some bags."

"Parker has bags, but is wondering why the fuck Hunter isn't helping," Parker's voice came from down the corridor.

"Hunter is wondering why the fuck Parker is talking about himself in third person." Hunter winked at me.

"You're doing it too," I said. I could hardly believe the guy standing in front of me was one of the Brantley twins. The last time I saw them, they couldn't have been more than fourteen. Awkward, gangly and full of mischief. The man standing in front of me now was tall and muscular. Still full of mischief, that much was obvious.

Parker stepped into the doorway, a bag in each hand. "Hey." He looked me up and down. "Little Mina DiMarco grew up."

If either of them were surprised by how thin I looked, they gave no indication. Given they weren't surprised to see me here, Reuben or Gianni must have filled them in.

"I was thinking the same about you," I said. "Are you still giving everyone hell?"

They gave me matching grins in response.

"We wouldn't be us if we didn't," Hunter said. "Some smartass, probably Zeke, decided to give us the nickname evil twins. We think it's hilarious."

I snorted softly. "I'm sure you do everything you can to live up to that."

Parker laughed. "I've always thought you were the smart one in your family. Not to mention the cute one." He hauled the bags over and placed them down on the floor beside me. "Reuben said you might need some new clothes. We did our best to max out his credit card."

"He trusts you with his credit card?" I did need new clothes, but I hadn't expected this. I probably should have, given that the twins' old clothes didn't fit that well.

"See, that's exactly what I think," Hunter said. "And yet, here we are." He spread his hands as though he was completely innocent.

"He's so full of shit," Parker said. "Reuben trusts *me* with his credit card, not Hunter."

Hunter turned to his twin and put a hand to his chest over his heart. "I'm shocked that you'd even suggest that, Park. Everyone knows I'm the trustworthy twin. As well as being the smartest and best looking."

"Keep telling yourself that, Hunter," Parker said.

I shook my head at them both and managed a smile. "I see you haven't changed a bit." They were still giving each other shit, but clearly adored each other. Whatever happened, they had each other's backs. What would it be like to grow up with someone you could trust implicitly?

"My cock is bigger," Parker said. He wiggled his eyebrows and grinned. "Hunter's stayed the same."

Hunter shouldered Parker hard enough to make him stagger a few steps. "What have I said about making unsubstantiated comments about my cock size?"

Parker shoved him back. "Fine, in the interests of accuracy, Hunter's got smaller."

"You're such an asshole," Hunter told him. He turned to me and said, "My cock is as big, if not bigger than Parker's. Any time you want to see, you only have to ask."

I cleared my throat. "Um, thanks. No offence but—"

They both groaned.

"Any time anyone says that, they're about to say something offensive," Hunter said.

"I was going to say that would be like looking at my younger brother's dick," I said.

They exchanged glances.

"I guess that wasn't so bad," Parker said.

Hunter nodded. "I can live with that. I mean, I don't *feel* offended."

I laughed softly. When was the last time I'd laughed?

A very long time ago. Knowing I hadn't completely forgotten how, was a relief.

"Thank you for the clothes," I said.

"I hope they fit," Parker said. "And that you didn't want anything in pink. I didn't get any pink." He frowned. "If you want pink, I can go and—" He gestured towards the door.

"I don't want any pink," I said quickly. "I actually prefer darker colours like black."

Parker dropped his hand to his thigh and grinned. "I got lots of black things. Black goes with everything."

"Especially my soul," Hunter said. "And Reuben's heart."

"What about my heart?" Reuben stepped into the library.

"Hunter was just saying you have a black heart," Parker said.

Reuben raised an eyebrow at them both, but didn't deny it. Nor did Hunter deny saying that about him.

"Don't you have somewhere to be?" Reuben asked, eyeing the twins meaningfully.

"At this exact moment, no," Hunter said. "That's why we're here, talking to Mina." He glanced at me. "You like books too? There might be room on Reuben's credit card for more books."

"I can't ask you to buy me things," I said.

"We like buying things," Parker said. "Especially if Reuben is paying."

"If you want books, you can have books," Reuben said to me.

I got the feeling that if I asked for the twin's heads on a silver platter, he'd give them to me. Fortunately for all concerned, that wasn't something I wanted or needed. On the contrary, it was difficult not to like Hunter and Parker. With them, there was no pretence. What you saw was what you got. I appreciated that.

"I...like romance books," I admitted with a shrug. The old Mina, before Kurt, believed in happily ever afters. That was probably why everyone believed my father's story that I ran off to get married. Behind every good lie was a dash of truth.

What did I believe now? Did it matter? I just wanted to lose myself in the pages for a little while. No one could blame me for that.

"Get her romance books," Reuben said to the twins. "Whatever she wants."

"As if you won't read them too," Hunter teased.

Reuben looked back at him, a bland expression on his face. "My library is missing having books with covers made from the hide of human male twins. I could have that rectified, if you like."

Hunter and Parker both laughed.

"You wouldn't do that to us," Parker said. "You love us too much."

Reuben grunted. "Don't tempt me." He nodded his dismissal and turned his back to them.

They both made faces at him behind his back, then

grinned at me before walking out of the room, their arms over each other's shoulders.

"Sometimes I wonder if they're adopted," Reuben said. "Then I remember, they're my half-brothers. It must be something from their mother's DNA."

"I envy them," I said softly. "They seem to love life."

Reuben sank into a chair and sighed heavily. "That they do. So should you." He pressed his lips together, then glanced down at the bags. "If you don't like anything in there, we can order more. Whatever you need."

I perched on the edge of another chair and reached for one of the bags.

"I need clothes, but if I open one of these and Kurt's head is inside…"

The sides of his eyes crinkled slightly, like he was holding back a smile. "We'd both thoroughly enjoy that. Unfortunately, we haven't found him yet. I have all of my resources on it. It won't be long. He can't hide from us forever."

At some point, I was going to have to use my own resources, but in the meantime I opened the bag and started to pull out various items of clothes. Mostly black trousers, black jeans, black skirts and lighter coloured blouses and T-shirts. Amongst those was lacy underwear in a variety of designs and sizes.

Every item looked expensive. The twins might not have exaggerated when they mentioned maxing out Reuben's credit card. Without access to my funds, I had little choice but to accept the extravagant gift. I'd draw more attention to myself dressed the way I was, than in the clothes stacked neatly in either of the bags.

"You didn't have to do this," I said, holding a black mohair jumper up to myself.

"You might prefer old track pants and T-shirts, but we'd soon run out of them," Reuben said dryly. "You'll feel more yourself in clothes of your own." His ice blue eyes regarded me intently, searching for my reaction, reading my response and taking note of everything.

For some reason, this was important to him, like he'd told the twins exactly what to buy. Like he'd chosen every item to make me look a certain way. The way he wanted me to look. This wasn't just about clothes, this was him making me into something. Moulding me into what he wanted. Claiming me in front of the world.

"I should try them on," I said. I stood and picked up both bags.

Reuben quickly rose too. "Do you need help?"

"I can manage," I said. Neither bag looked too heavy. If they were, I might have refused his help anyway. This was a small thing, but I needed to do it by myself. To prove to myself I wasn't a broken doll. "Thank you."

"It was my pleasure," he said, his voice smoother than silk. He'd be thinking of every centimetre of fabric as it slid against my skin, touching me in a way he wanted to, but couldn't. Not yet. If I was, *when* I was, ready to give myself to a man, he'd be ready. Ready to fill me, touch me. Claim me.

"Breakfast will be served soon," he said. "If you're up to eating."

He looked indifferent to the idea of food, as though he only ate because he had to, not because he cared about cuisine. What did he care about, apart from books and his family?

If the twins were open books, Reuben was one whose pages were shut tight and locked, the key hidden from the world. What would it take to break that lock? Why did I want to? He intrigued me. Many people found him intimidating, but I never had. To me, I saw a complicated man behind a stony façade. A mystery to be solved.

There was more to him than just a callous mobster, although he was undeniably that too. He'd have people killed without a second thought, but he's always looked at me like I was also a puzzle he wanted to figure out.

I hadn't realised until now that we were so alike.

"I am," I agreed. "I won't be long." Especially now I realised the smell of bacon was wafting through the house. It was good enough to make my mouth water, even as my stomach twinged in warning.

He sat back in his chair and nodded. "I'll wait for you in the kitchen in about ten minutes."

I nodded quickly and turned to make my way back up the stairs, one careful step at a time.

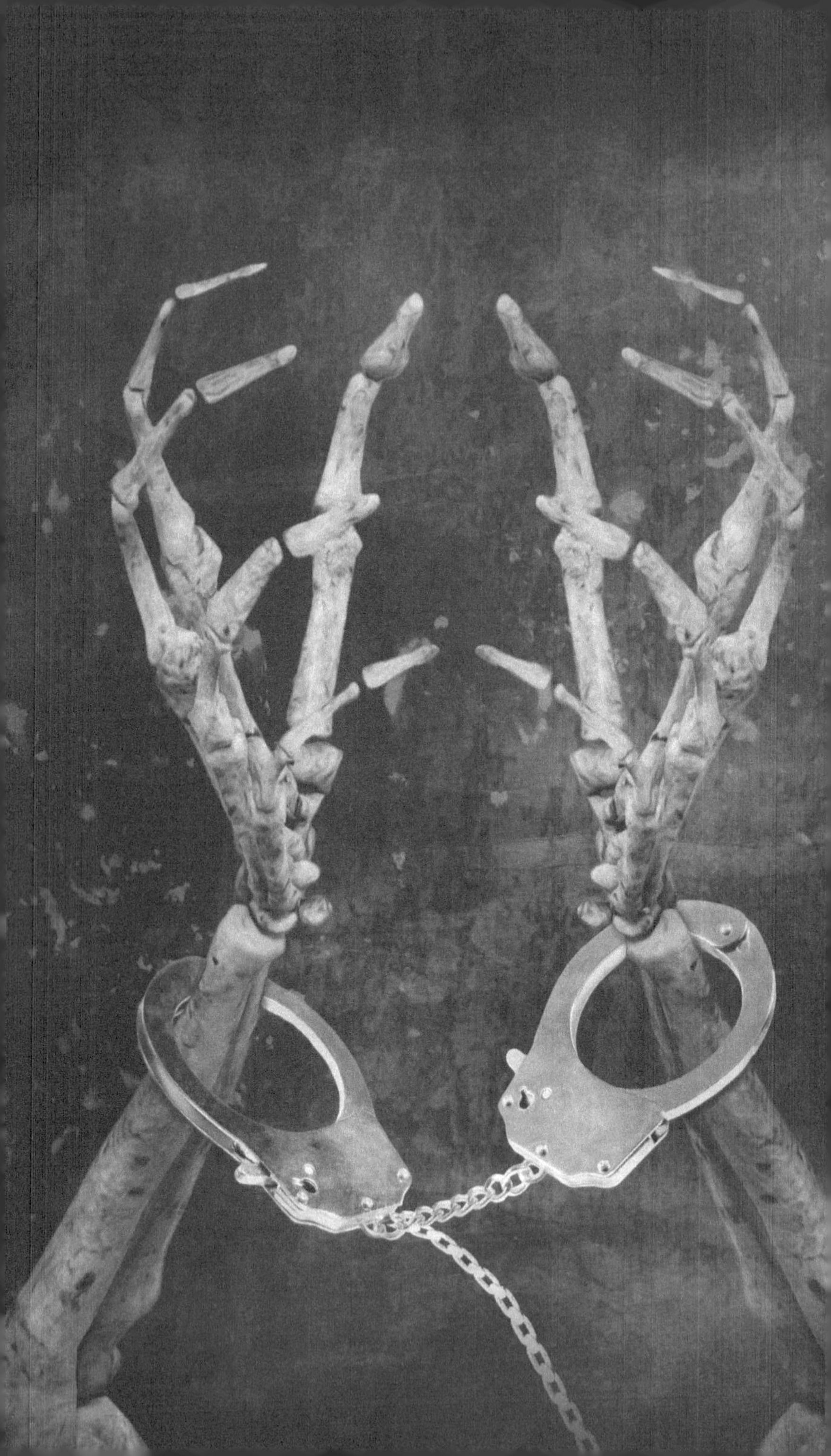

CHAPTER 10

REUBEN

If I was ever going to slam my fist down onto a tabletop, it would be now.

Inside, my blood was boiling. I kept it contained, kept my exterior calm, if tense.

"Even if Kurt Lasalle was dead, we should be able to find him," I said. "No one disappears off the face of the fucking planet unless we have a hand in it."

"It's possible Samuel Bell or someone else dealt with him," Damon said.

"If Bell did, he'd leave tracks in the sand deeper than his asshole," Gianni said.

I grimaced at that analogy. Bell didn't have the finesse we did, but the last place I wanted my thoughts to go was his asshole.

"Is there any chance he convinced his sister to harbour him?" I asked.

I didn't want to have to deal with Daisy, or Mina's

cousin Ric, but if they were hiding Kurt, I'd have no choice. I suspected if they were, Mina wouldn't want me to be gentle with her cousin either. Not if he was complicit in what happened to her. It wouldn't matter if he was her cousin or a complete stranger. She'd want his head in a bag beside Kurt's.

Her comment about finding his disembodied head instead of clothes made my blood surge and my balls take notice.

There was something incredibly arousing about women who liked revenge. She was completely serious about wanting to see him dead in front of her. She wouldn't have flinched. At least, she wouldn't regret it if he was dead.

Seeing a part of him, without warning, may have served as a trigger. One that no one in this room would have blamed her for. No, we'd hold her close while Kurt's blood seeped into a puddle on the hardwood floor.

Damon shook his head. "I spoke to Caleb this morning. He said there's no way in hell Daisy would protect her brother. She was pissed when she found out what he did."

Caleb was probably pissed at getting a call from Damon instead of me. The second oldest in the family, my brother tended to believe in his own importance. He was useful, or he wouldn't have the responsibilities he did, but sometimes he came too close to overstepping.

I nodded slowly in response. "We have contracts out

on Kurt?" I knew the answer, but I asked the question anyway.

"Every mercenary, hitman and assassin," Damon said. "All vying for a substantial amount of money." He'd questioned the need to offer that much, but I insisted. I would have offered double if it meant Kurt was found faster. Triple. I'd stipulated that he was to be brought in alive. His death was a last resort.

"I bet the Sparrow would have found him," Gianni drawled. "If anyone could, they could."

I grunted my agreement. When they were active, the Sparrow was one of the most skilled and feared assassins in the business. No one knew who they were, including me, which still irritated me after so long. No one knew why they'd gone inactive either.

They took a job a few years back, completed it and disappeared. Speculation was rife, as was to be expected. Maybe the Sparrow was dead. Maybe they made enough money to retire and were living quietly in a house beside a forest, where there were no people around for days.

If that was the case, I envied them. I owned a house like that, but didn't go there nearly enough. Maybe now I would, since I had more reason to spend time there. I could show Mina the place. I had a feeling she'd love the calm, the nature, the roaring fire in the massive fireplace. It was the perfect place to stop, think and just be.

"Given we don't have help from the Sparrow, we'll have to rely on what resources we do have," I said.

I glanced up as Mina stopped in the doorway leading into the kitchen. My breath left my body.

She was dressed in black jeans and a tank top in a shade of red so dark it almost looked black. Everything was slightly loose, giving her room to fill into it, but the sight of her still sent a surge of blood to my cock.

If I ever had a wet dream, it would feature her, just like this. I wanted to peel off every layer slowly, revealing her skin, scars and all.

I wanted to suck both of her nipples, the perfect one and the one Kurt tried so hard to destroy. I didn't care what they looked like, every part of her was mine. I wanted to touch her everywhere. To show her how beautiful she was, how strong.

"I'll get you food." Gianni leapt up from the table before I could finish taking a breath.

She turned to him and offered the smallest of smiles. "Not too much."

He picked up a plate and glanced back to grin. "Definitely no overdoing it this time."

He placed a piece of toast and a rasher of bacon on her plate before putting it down beside his spot. He poured her a cup of tea and placed it down before pulling out a chair for her.

I held back a growl. Not because I should have been doing those things for her, but because she seemed so determined to do those things for herself. He shouldn't be trying to undermine her. Lucky for him, she didn't seem to mind him helping right now.

She sat graciously and picked up her toast to nibble on the corner.

Gianni plonked himself back in his chair and resumed eating his own breakfast.

"We were just saying we haven't found Kurt yet," I told her.

"We're still looking," Damon said. "We'll find him." He seemed to take Kurt's continued ability to evade us, personally. Not for Mina's sake, but because he was one of the best. He hated to be shown up, especially by a prick like Lasalle.

"Hell yeah, we will," Gianni said. "Terry, this bacon is perfection."

Terry, who stood at the sink washing a pan, nodded to acknowledge that Gianni spoke. He was a man of even fewer words than me. He looked as though he'd punch the crap out of someone with one hand while sipping his coffee with the other. As far as I knew, the only thing he ever broke was eggs. Every so often, I'd send him out with one of the others to intimidate someone who deserved it. That usually got the job done quicker. They didn't know Terry wouldn't hurt a hair on their head. If anything, I think he found the whole thing funny.

I watched Mina as she picked up her own piece of bacon and bit off the end. She closed her eyes and sighed like it was pure bliss.

I pictured her mouth around my cock, the same expression on her face. I was a patient man, I'd wait until she was ready before I slipped my head between her lips and fucked her mouth.

My grip on my coffee cup tightened. If it wasn't for Kurt fucking Lasalle, we wouldn't have to wait. I could have her on her knees right now, licking, sucking, tasting me when I came down her throat.

Gianni made a sound in the back of his own throat like he was thinking the same thing.

Damon was staring at her too.

As if she suddenly became aware of the scrutiny, her eyes popped open. She looked around at all of us, shrinking back with self-consciousness.

"It's really good bacon," she whispered.

"It's the best fucking bacon ever," Gianni said.

"It's not bad bacon," Damon said.

Terry grunted.

Damon smirked. "Fine, it's great bacon, okay?"

"Lucky you said that," Gianni told him. "Terry has been known to stab people with a fork for less." He slid a sly glance in Terry's direction.

Terry gave him the side eye in return.

"No he hasn't," Damon said evenly.

"Okay, no he hasn't, but there's a first time for everything." Gianni shrugged and grinned.

I watched Mina as she listened to them banter back and forth. Her eyes were wide, but she seemed amused. What would it take to make her smile or laugh?

The answer to that was one reason I was willing to accept if she wanted to be with Gianni too. He could make her laugh and smile where I couldn't. Those were things that came easier to him than they did to me. I could buy her things, I could make her look the way I wanted, I could satisfy her in ways she hadn't begun to understand, but I wasn't the clown he and the twins were. I never would be. I didn't want to be. I wanted to give her everything I could offer, not the things I couldn't.

She looked back at me as she continued to nibble carefully on her bacon. From the look in her blue-green eyes, she knew exactly what was going on inside my head somehow. Or at least, on the surface and she wanted to dig down deeper.

I wanted her to do exactly that, but it would have to happen gradually. As long as I could remember, I'd had walls up higher than those around a prison yard. No one had gone past them. Few people wanted to. Fewer people were *allowed* to. I couldn't take the risk of letting them in, I didn't want to.

The only person I ever wanted to see the real me was her.

Had I been so guarded for so long I didn't know how to let her in either? That was going to be my battle. That and making sure she knew she belonged to me. Whatever it took, I wouldn't step aside from her. The only way anyone would take her from me was if I was dead. Or she was. If anyone tried to kill her, they'd be the ones to end up dead. Slowly and painfully.

"I heard you say something about the Sparrow," she

said. She finished her bacon and licked the tips of her fingers in a way that had all three of us staring again.

Fuck. This woman and her tongue. My cock was throbbing so hard it almost hurt. I wanted to feel that warm, wet tongue circling my tip, teasing me.

I cleared my throat. "That's right, we were," I said. "The Sparrow was an assassin. Or maybe a shadow."

She frowned at that. "A shadow?"

It was Damon who responded. "No one knew anything about them. They accepted a job, got it done and took the money. People tried to hunt them down, but never found them."

"Isn't that the job of an assassin?" she asked.

"The Sparrow got into places no one else could," Gianni said. "Places no one should have been able to get into. No one knows how."

"Precisely," Damon said. "People have spent years trying to figure it out. Some speculate the Sparrow used some special technology, and some suggest they were a ghost. Some people even say there was more than one. That it was two people who worked together."

"What do you think?" She picked up her tea and took a sip. There was no groan of appreciation now, but she seemed to enjoy the taste.

Damon shrugged. "I think they were very fucking good at what they did."

"Damon is jealous of their skills," Gianni said.

"So are you," Damon said flatly.

"Fucking right I am," Gianni agreed. "I'm too tall to

sneak around like that. And too outgoing." He flipped his short ponytail.

"You mean too loud," Damon said. "You'd be playing metal music so loud, everyone would hear you coming from a week away."

Mina shuddered at the mention of music, but took another sip before putting her cup back down. "I think I've had enough for now."

"You're doing well," I told her. "Good girl." I didn't miss the way her eyes widened at that. Or the way my dick throbbed a little harder.

Waiting might be more difficult than I thought.

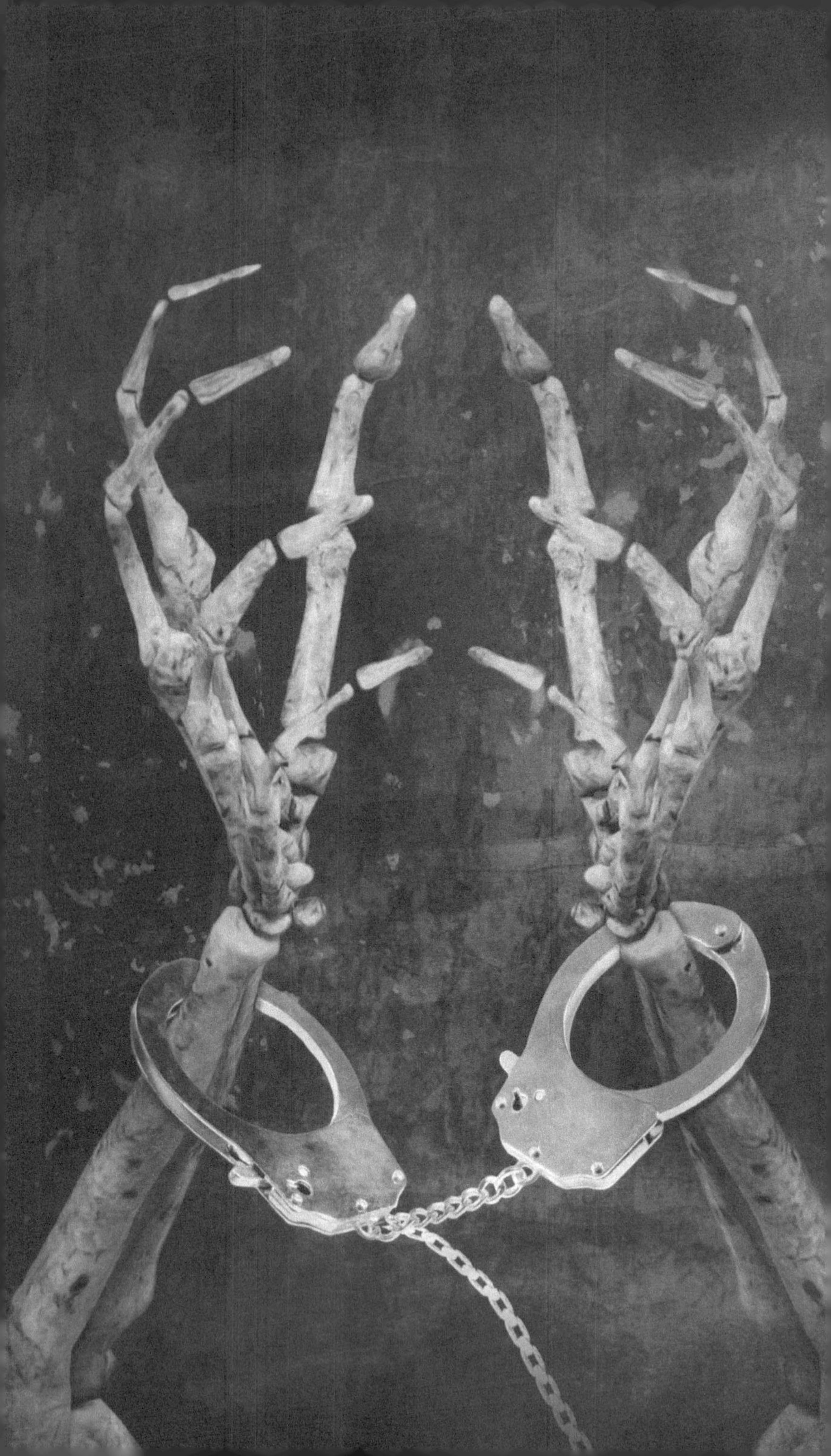

CHAPTER 11

MINA

I looked up from the book I was reading, a romantic comedy about ice hockey players, to see Gianni step into the room.

His gaze swept over me, followed by a smile. "Morning, sweetheart. Guess what?"

"Asher would have responded to that with, 'You're mad and I'm not.'" I closed the book.

Gianni chuckled. "He might have been right there. But no, that wasn't what I was going to say. We have a lead on Kurt." He looked like a kid who was let loose in a chocolate shop.

I stood up so quickly the book slid off my lap and onto the floor. I shook off a wave of dizziness and leaned over to scoop up the book.

"We found him?" I asked. I placed the book on the table beside the chair and clasped my trembling hands.

"Not yet," Gianni said. "But we found some

associates of his. We're on our way to have a friendly conversation with them."

"I'm coming," I said immediately. I'd been here for a couple of weeks and felt a lot stronger already. My clothes fit better and I could move up and down the stairs faster. I could do this too.

He grinned. "I was hoping you'd say that. If Reuben or Damon say you can't come, I'll set them straight."

"Or I will," I said. The way he took care of me was sweet, but I was better able to stand on my own two feet each day. Literally and figuratively.

"Or that," he agreed, his smile unwavering. "Between us, we'll make sure you can come along." He offered me his hand.

I looked down at it for a few moments before slipping my hand into his. Touching another person didn't feel as uncomfortable as it had. The idea didn't make me break out into a cold sweat as easily. His respect for my boundaries led me to expanding them, bit by bit.

We walked down to the back of the house, to the door that led to the garage. Reuben was already there, dressed impeccably as always.

Damon stood beside him, checking over his gun.

They both looked up when Gianni and I approached.

"This isn't the time for—" Damon started.

"I'm coming with you," I said firmly. I slid my hand out of Gianni's and crossed my arms over my chest.

They were all taller than me, but I wasn't going to let myself be intimidated. Not by them nor anyone else.

Reuben closed his eyes tightly for a few moments, before opening them and nodding. "If any of us tell you to do *anything*, including wait in the car, you obey. Understood?"

"Within reason," I said. "I'm not some sort of delicate flower."

He looked at me like he thought that was exactly what I was. Delicate anyway, if not a flower.

"I'll decide what's within reason or not." He nodded to Damon, who led the way out to one of the cars, a dark SUV.

Like when they brought me here, Damon and Reuben took their places in the front, Gianni and me in the back.

"It's been a long time since we've been on a road trip," Gianni said.

"We've never been on a road trip." Damon backed the car out of the garage and onto the road.

Gianni snapped his fingers, making me flinch slightly. "That's right. We should go on one sometime. Just for shits and giggles."

"Being in a car with you for hours on end would definitely give us the shits," Damon remarked.

"And giggles," Gianni said with a grin.

I shook my head at both of them. "Who are these people we're going to have a conversation with?"

Reuben sighed. "It seems Lasalle had his own

network for running drugs and weapons. It's a lot more extensive than we suspected."

He sounded beyond irritated. Not just because Kurt was operating behind his back, but because somehow they missed the extent of it. He was the kind of man who didn't like to overlook anything. He wanted to be aware of everything that went on in his proximity, and way beyond it.

"How extensive?" I asked.

"Extensive enough," Reuben said. "We'll be making an example of them. After we learn what they know."

I leaned back and left it at that for now. What mattered to me was finding Kurt.

We sat in silence except for Gianni occasionally humming some random tune I couldn't recognise. Not the one he played for me the other night. He hadn't tried to play any more music for me after that. If I stepped into a room while he had any on, he quickly turned it off.

I didn't remark on it. No matter what I would have said, he would have done it anyway.

We drove for maybe thirty minutes, before pulling into a side road. Damon stopped the car in front of what looked like an ice cream parlour, and killed the engine.

"According to my sources, this was a front," Damon said.

"I like it," Gianni said. "No one would suspect an ice cream parlour." He steepled his fingers and pressed them to his lips. "Why didn't we think of this?"

"Because we already have a winery, several restaurants and a car wash," Damon said. "Those assets are sufficient and more profitable."

"But much less *fun* than an ice cream parlour," Gianni said. "Except the winery."

"If I ever decide to invest in one, you can run it," Reuben said dryly.

I wasn't sure if he was serious or not.

Gianni grinned. "Promise? Actually, I don't want to run it, but I will frequent it. Maybe the twins can run it. That sounds more like their jam."

Reuben smirked and pushed his door open to get out of the car.

I followed close behind, anxiety starting to get the better of me. I pushed it down. Reminded myself who I was. Chances were, Kurt wouldn't be here. He'd spent the last couple of weeks lying low, he wasn't going to stick around if he got wind of us coming.

What if he didn't? I asked myself. What if he had no idea we were here? We could walk right through the front door of the ice cream parlour and find him sitting there, eating a sundae. The kind with chocolate sauce and a sprinkling of nuts.

Before the anxiety became a full-blown panic attack, one of the twins stepped out of the front of the building.

Of course. Reuben wasn't walking through the front door without anyone knowing he was coming. The closer we got, the more of his people I saw inside, surrounding several men and one woman, who sat on the floor in the middle of the parlour. Each had a gun pointed at their head.

Reuben was the boss, he would have sent people here the minute he got word of Kurt's involvement. Possibly hours ago. They would have secured the area before he stepped foot out of his house.

That meant two things: I was safe here, and Kurt wasn't present. That didn't mean we couldn't learn his whereabouts.

I followed Reuben and Damon into the building.

Damon slid a side-eye glance at Gianni, when Gianni peered at the tubs of ice cream behind the glass panel.

Gianni grinned and turned his attention to the people who sat on the floor, taking in each one with interest.

It was an act, I realised. Pretending to be more interested in the ice cream than the people who worked for Kurt. He was letting them think he was harmless, nice even. For him, they might let their guard down. The truth was, he was more dangerous than Reuben and Damon. Subtler.

Reuben nodded for an older man to be brought forward. Two of his men grabbed him and dragged him closer.

"None of them have been helpful," Hunter said. At least, I thought it was him.

"Depending on your definition of helpful," Parker

said. "A couple have promised to tell us everything, in return for keeping their toes."

"What Parker said," Hunter said. "But if any of them know where Kurt is, they're keeping their mouths shut."

"I swear on anything you want me to swear on, I have no idea where he is." The man at Reuben's feet looked up at him with begging eyes. "He hasn't been here in three weeks, maybe four." He glanced over his shoulder.

"Lionel is right," the woman said. She was the calmest of them all. "He rarely came here himself."

I took a step back. Gianni put out a hand to steady me. I shook my head. "I'm okay. I just…" I stared at the woman. I'd never seen her before, but I knew that voice.

"He didn't come here because you went to him," I said.

She turned a gaze on me that was so cold it was brittle.

Reuben's look was slightly warmer. "She went to him?"

"One of the voices I heard above the basement was hers," I said. "I heard it several times. She worked for him. She knew where that house was."

Damon had his gun out, aiming at her. The twins had theirs trained on her too.

"Did you know about the basement?" Reuben asked, an underlying warning in his tone. Warning of what, I wasn't sure. If she knew about the basement, she was dead. If she didn't…

I couldn't guess what he'd order to be done with her.

She looked confused. "What basement? All I know is that I went to one address to keep him updated with the operation here. Benny went too, at different times." She jerked her head towards another man, his hair cropped close to his scalp.

"You never went down into the basement?" Gianni asked. "I thought that was where Kurt kept all the weapons?" He spoke lightly, like maybe Kurt kept pinball machines down there or something.

"We were never allowed down there," Benny said.

All the guns were now pointed at him.

"Oh, you knew about the basement," Gianni said with a smile. "Did he tell you why you weren't allowed down there?"

Benny's eyes shifted back and forth. He swallowed physically.

Hunter cocked his gun. "Answer the question."

"He once said something about keeping someone down there," Benny said, his voice high. "He didn't say that to me, I overheard him talking to someone else. He laughed about it. I thought maybe…maybe he was trafficking women and kept them down there. It was none of my business."

"You never thought to check, in case there was something else going on?" Damon asked. "He might have had his mother down there."

"Like I said, it was none of my business." Benny raised his chin defiantly. "I wasn't paid to stick my nose into his personal business. If a guy wants to keep his mother in the basement, that's up to him."

I flinched at the sound of a gunshot and a spray of blood and brains. The back half of Benny's head was gone before he slumped down onto the floor.

"Oops," Hunter said. "My finger slipped."

"If yours hadn't, mine would have," Parker said. "What sort of asshole doesn't care if another asshole has his mother in the basement?"

"A dead one," Damon said. He looked around at the remaining prisoners, most of whom were cowering together. "Anyone else want to supply some useful information?" He raised his eyebrow at the woman who seemed to know more than the rest.

While silence fell, my eyes went to Benny. His eyes were open, staring. I should have been horrified, but I'd seen enough death that it hadn't bothered me, not for a long time. If anything, the idea of someone who might have been able to help me, but didn't, lying dead near my feet was arousing. Almost as much as if I'd done it myself.

I looked back up and locked eyes with the other woman. She tried to look away, but not before I saw something in her expression.

"You knew, didn't you?" I said softly. I was vaguely aware of everyone turning to me. "I don't just recognise your voice from hearing it above me. I heard it before that. When I was drugged and taken down there.

People carried me and you were giving them orders to do it."

"Orders on Kurt's behalf," she said calmly.

"You still followed them," I said. I took a step towards her. "You knew I was there the whole time and you did *nothing*. You knew what he was doing to me."

"I had an idea," she said. She offered no further explanation.

"Fucking hell," someone whispered. I thought it might have been Parker.

"Damon—" Reuben started.

I put up my hand towards him. "No. Gianni." I held out my other hand until he placed a knife across my fingers. I curled my hand around the hilt, feeling the familiar, cool steel.

I took a step forward towards the woman.

The twins took steps back, but their guns remained trained on her head. They didn't need to. The woman didn't flinch as I sliced open her throat.

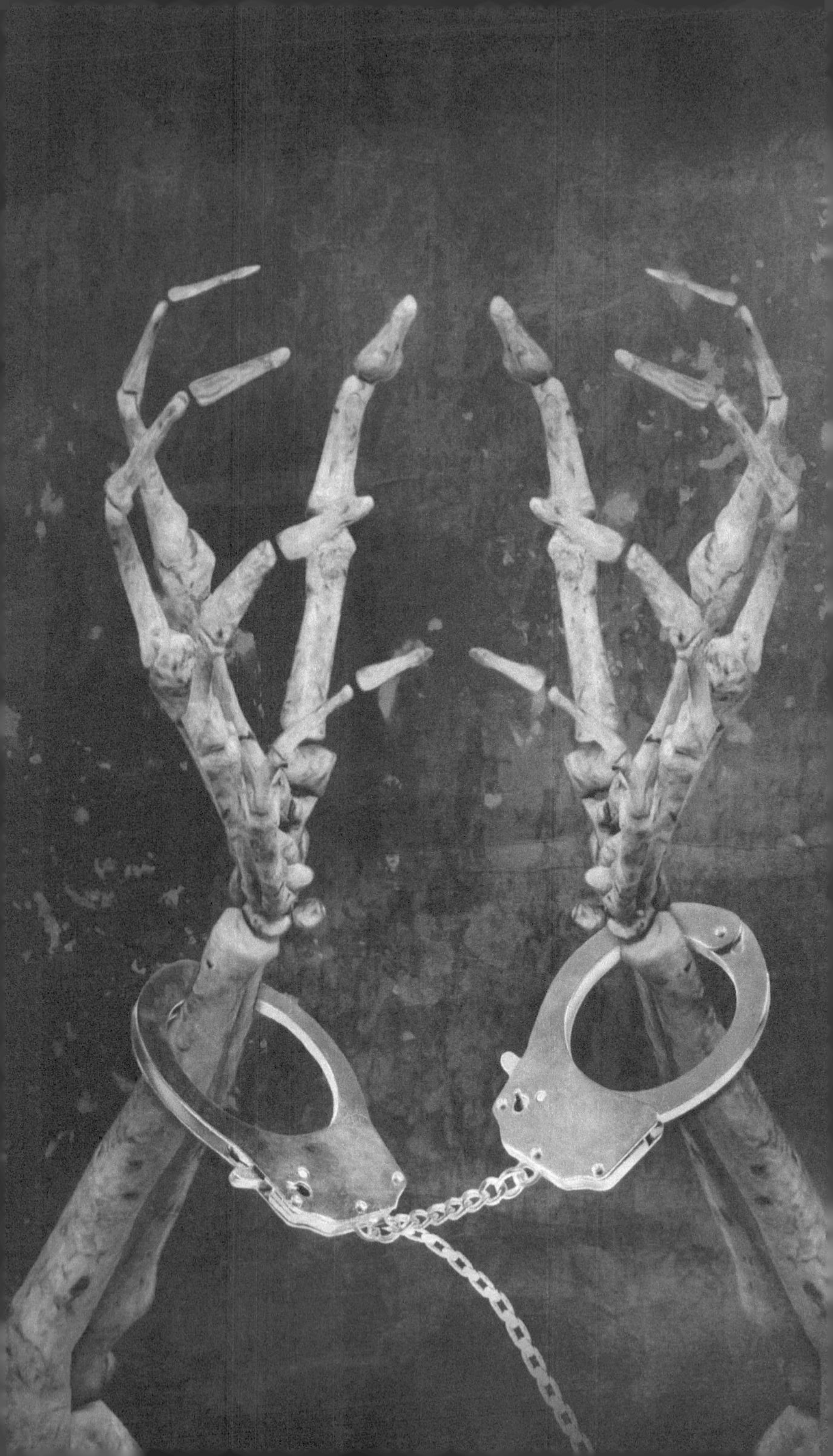

CHAPTER 12

REUBEN

"That was fucking hot," Gianni said softly.

I grunted my agreement. I was aware that Mina had some steel in her, but I hadn't expected her to use it to kill a woman. When she insisted Damon and I back off, I thought she was going to threaten her.

I should have known better. At the end of the day, she was a DiMarco. She was as much a part of this life as I was. And she was fucking angry at what they did to her.

Right now though, she looked small, her expression blank. She still had blood on her hand and up her arm. After killing the woman, she'd staggered back, the knife falling from her fingers. Her face was white, like she might faint. Instead, she sat in a chair and barely moved since.

I took the washcloth Parker handed me and

crouched down in front of Mina to wipe away the blood from her fingers.

"I should have realised there was a chance someone like that might be here."

"I'm glad she was," Mina whispered. "She let me live down there for years, and didn't raise a finger. She probably didn't even think about me and what he was doing to me."

A frown crossed her brow. "Or maybe she did, and she didn't speak out because he might have put her down there instead. She'd rather let someone else suffer through that than go through it herself."

"She could have told me and no one would have gone through it." I turned her hand to wipe her palm clean. "She chose not to do that."

Mina looked down at me. "I had my doubts at first. That it was her. It could have been someone else's voice."

"Until she confirmed that she knew what happened to you," I said.

Mina nodded. "Until then. Before that, I wanted to kill her for working with him. I would have let one of you shoot her."

"And we would have," I said. "I would have ordered one of them to put a bullet in her brain."

"What if I was wrong?" Mina asked. "What if it wasn't her upstairs? You could have had an innocent woman killed."

I wiped Mina's wrist. "There are many adjectives for

a woman like her. Innocent isn't amongst them. Whether or not she knew about you, she was still working with him. Any chance of her walking out of here alive were slim. Less than slim. I always intended to make an example out of the people here. I won't tolerate people working for Kurt or anyone like him. I won't tolerate rival operations, especially ones as big as his."

"Right," she whispered. "But what if you planned to let them walk away and I asked you to kill her, and then I was wrong?"

"Why are you asking this?" I asked. "If you asked me to kill her, you would have had good reason to do it." And if she didn't, I didn't give a shit. If she wanted someone dead, they were dead. Innocent or not.

"I just…" She glanced down at the floor. "I don't want to make a mistake." She looked like she was going to say 'again,' but didn't.

"What they did to you wasn't your fault," I stated. "It was your father's fault. Him and Kurt. And hers." I didn't so much as jerk my head towards the woman's corpse. She didn't deserve that much attention or recognition.

"And others. You mentioned several people carried you down there. Would you recognise any of them?"

She breathed in slowly through her nose and blew out through pursed lips. "I don't know. Maybe."

I finished wiping away the blood and tossed the washcloth aside. "How are you feeling?"

"About killing someone?" she asked. "If I'm supposed to say I regret it, I can't. I..." In a whisper she said, "I enjoyed it. They say violence isn't the answer, but..."

"Sometimes it's the only answer," I said. I noticed the way her eyes got darker when she talked about what she did. She more than enjoyed killing, she got off on it. She wasn't the first person to feel that way. Or the last.

I looked back over my shoulder. "Kill the rest of them," I said calmly. Even if they weren't working for Kurt, they saw Mina and Hunter kill. I wasn't leaving any witnesses behind.

I turned back to her, ignoring the pleas for me to change my mind. They were cut off by three gunshots. Quickly and efficiently, my people did as they were asked, before dragging the bodies out into the back of the building to be disposed of.

We'd done this so many times before, everyone knew their role and carried it out without hesitation.

"All of this death shouldn't be, I don't know..." Mina frowned.

"Loud?" I suggested. I was as uncomfortable with the sound of gunshots as I was with screaming. Not because I cared about the implications; because of the noise.

"I was going to say exciting," she said tentatively. "We got to decide who lived and died here today. We did that."

"Yes we did," I agreed. "That's one of the benefits of

being the boss. You get to make those choices." I'd made them so often in the last few years I barely gave them a second thought. Speaking to her reminded me how much I enjoyed the power. I liked things done my way. My way made sense to me. Neat, orderly and organised.

"Some people would suggest we're fucked up," she said.

"What do you think?" I was genuinely curious as to how she saw herself and our lifestyle.

"I think it's who we are," she said. "Who we'll always be."

She understood. This was exactly what I'd been trying to tell Zeke for years now. This was who he was as well. He could try to put it behind him, but he never would. Not completely.

I'd never wanted to kiss her more than I did right then. I wanted to slam my lips down on hers and claim her right here, in front of everyone, beside pools of blood on the tiled floor. Was there a more appropriate setting?

I settled for placing a small kiss on the centre of her forehead. "You're so fucking beautiful."

"Because I'm fucked up?" she asked.

"You said 'perfect as fuck' wrong," Gianni said, crouching beside me. "I've never had the hots for a woman like I do right now. Seeing you kill that bitch was spank bank material."

I looked at him sideways and arched an eyebrow.

"Don't say you don't agree," he said.

"It was the wording I was questioning," I said. He sounded like the twins, using an expression like spank bank. Mina deserved better than to be talked about like that.

Admittedly, I didn't have a better term for it. I would be thinking about her when I curled my hand around my cock later tonight.

Gianni grinned. "What can I say, I'm classy as fuck. That's why you love me so much."

How could I respond to that but to roll my eyes and shake my head.

"Boss, the cleanup is finished," Damon said. "We just need to get someone in here to wash up the blood. I've already made the call." He stopped beside us to regard Mina. His expression was one of grudging respect, with a healthy dose of heat.

He'd be the last to admit it, but he felt the same way about her as Gianni and me. Right now, he was all professionalism as he pushed his expressionless mask back into place.

"Good." I rose to my feet, taking Mina with me, my hand gripping hers. "Keep an eye on this place. Kurt might return. If he doesn't, someone else who works for him will."

"Got it, boss," Damon said.

Gianni pushed himself to his feet. "I have to admit to being disappointed. Not only did we not find out where Kurt was, I didn't get to kill anyone. Although, watching Mina kill someone was almost as much fun. Maybe we can do it again sometime. A good date night isn't complete without a few corpses."

"Try to keep the killing to a minimum," I told him. "Unless they're involved with Kurt." Then he had free reign to deal with them however he saw fit. I knew I could trust him to be discreet and clean up after himself. And that he'd let me know whoever he killed, in great detail. He enjoyed giving those reports almost as much as doing the actual deed. His eyes always glazed like he was reliving the moment, step-by-step.

I also knew he didn't go around killing indiscriminately. It wasn't the death he enjoyed dispensing, it was the justice.

"I'll do my best," he said easily. He took half a step away before he stopped and frowned at Mina. "What's wrong?"

She stood with her back completely straight, frozen to the spot, staring at nothing in particular in front of her.

"If I hadn't acted so quickly, we might have been able to get her to tell us who else was with her that night," Mina said. "I screwed up."

Her face was paler again. Her blue-green eyes and dark hair were a stark contrast against her skin, almost making her look ghostly. Beautiful, but haunted.

I took the chance of putting an arm around her shoulders. When she didn't pull away, I squeezed lightly. "Chances are, she wouldn't have told you anything else. She already knew her time was done. I doubt she would have thrown anyone else under the bus."

"She was quick to point out Benny's involvement," Gianni said.

"I screwed up," Mina said again. "I screwed up. I screwed up." She put her hands over her face and pressed the heels into her eyes like she was trying to rub them out of her head.

I grabbed her wrists and pulled her hands down. "You did *not* screw up," I said firmly. "We will find the others if they're still alive. We'll make them pay for what they did to you. I promise you that. We'll find them."

Her eyes were wide as she looked back at me. A brief moment of confusion crossed her face before she blinked and stopped trying to pull away from me. I had the distinct impression she'd gotten lost in the past somehow. Whatever had her upset went beyond cutting the woman's throat today. Something happened that haunted her, something that had nothing to do with Kurt.

"We'll find them," she whispered.

"Yes," I said. "When we do, they'll get what they deserve."

She shivered. "What they deserve," she echoed. "Yes, they should get that. Everything that's coming to them."

I couldn't shake the feeling she was talking about herself.

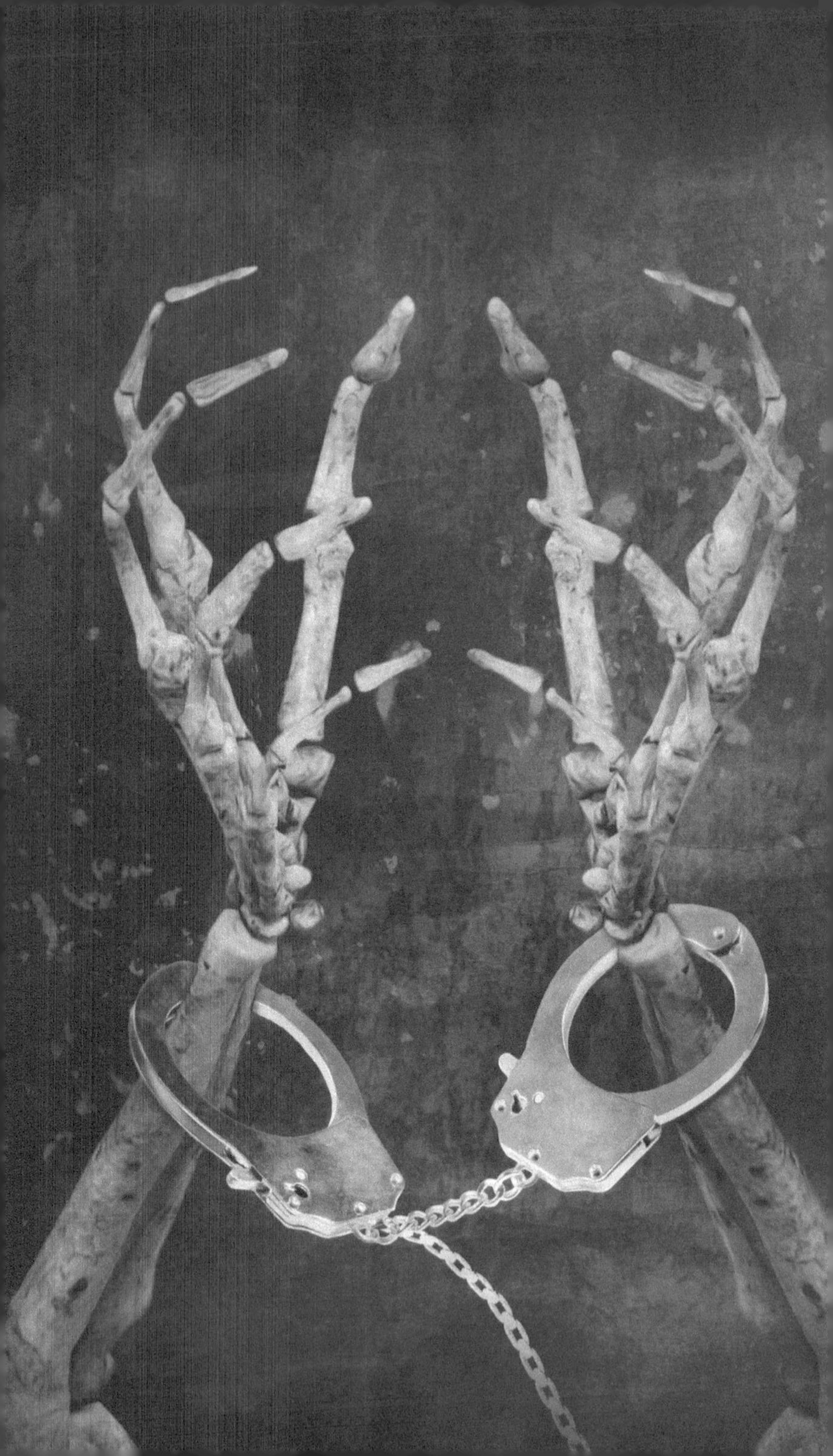

CHAPTER 13

MINA

I pulled on silky pyjama pants and a sleep singlet and sat down on my bed, my back against the pillows.

My hand still tingled from where Reuben cleaned the blood off my skin. I could still feel his touch long after the blood dried. So gentle and thorough, right before he ordered the deaths of several people.

Some would call him a monster, but my whole body throbbed in a way I hadn't felt in the longest time. Chained up in that cage, the last thing on my mind was intimacy or arousal. All of my attention was occupied with surviving.

Now, with time to think about other things, I could dwell on killing that woman.

I acted out of anger. That was the worst thing I could have done. I was trained to be cool, calm and rational. Not furious and rash. In spite of Reuben, Gianni and

Damon's reassurances, I was regretful, my anger now turned inward to myself.

After a brief tap on the door, it swung inward and Reuben stepped inside. He wore black trousers and a dark grey button down, folded to his elbows. This seemed to be as casual as he ever got. I suspected he didn't own a pair of jeans or even a T-shirt. What would it take to convince him to try either of those?

He was handsome and compelling, especially with those intense, ice blue eyes. He also had the muscles to pull off a T-shirt and make women stare. Men too.

He didn't wait for an invitation. He closed the door behind him and stepped over to sit on the side of the bed.

"Have you come to tell me again that I shouldn't blame myself?" I asked. "Because you can say whatever you want I'm still going to—"

"I didn't." He spoke in a voice that was both deep and as compelling as his eyes. "I saw your reaction to killing that woman. And to Hunter killing that other man." He seemed to be hunting for his name, but couldn't remember.

"Benny," I supplied.

He hummed his agreement in the back of his throat. "They tend to blur together after a while. That's not important. What's important is you. What you were feeling at the time."

"Are we having a therapy session?" I asked lightly.

He choked back a soft laugh. "Fuck no. Not exactly."

"Then what?" I asked. "I wasn't bothered by seeing them die. I've seen enough death that it doesn't get to me anymore."

He tilted his head back and looked over at me. "I think we both know that's not true. It does get to you. You like it. Death turns you on."

His words left me breathless for a couple of heartbeats. Of all the things people ever said to me, this was the first time I felt as though anyone actually understood me. More than that, he looked at me with absolutely no judgement. No, whatever he thought about this, he wasn't judging me for it.

"I never said I wasn't fucked up," I said.

He made no move towards me. Or away. "You're not fucked up. Everyone has things that arouse them. It's what we do with them that matters."

"You've come to share what gets you off?" I asked.

One of his eyebrows twitched. "This isn't about me. This is about you and what you need."

"And what do I need?" I whispered. The idea of being touched was terrifying, but the way my pussy reacted to his presence, to the memory of warm blood all over my hand, I needed something.

"I'm guessing you didn't touch yourself when you were in that cage," he said.

"Not...not like that," I said. I glanced down at the bed covers.

"What about before that?"

I looked back up at him. "Before that I did. I mean, I was, you know…"

"A normal eighteen-year-old woman?" His jaw clenched, clearly furious at my father and Kurt for stealing those years from me.

"If you could call me normal," I said lightly. I didn't think there was much normal about me back then, but compared to now I supposed I was.

"What did you think about?" he asked. "When you touched yourself."

I thought back. "I don't know. Guys I knew. Book boyfriends. You."

A flicker of surprise crossed his face. "Me?"

Should I have said that? I couldn't take it back now. His raised eyebrow was a clear insistence that I explain.

"Why not you? You're strong, powerful and handsome. Dangerous. Like an open fire a girl shouldn't step into."

"But you wanted to?" His eyes darkened in a way that, under other circumstances, in another lifetime, I might have peeled off my clothes and begged him to fuck me.

"Yes," I said simply.

"Touch yourself," he whispered. "I want to see you."

I swallowed. "It's been so long."

"Exactly. You deserve to know your body belongs to you." He looked like he was about to add 'and me,' but held the words back for now. "Touch yourself."

I slipped my hand down between my legs and

lightly ran the tips of my fingers over the front of my pyjama pants.

My eyes on his, I ran them up and down, barely touching the fabric, or my pussy underneath them. It felt good. Better than good. It felt as though a part of me was slowly coming back to life. That maybe I could put what Kurt did behind me. If I wasn't ready for a man to touch me, there was no reason I couldn't give myself pleasure. And give it to Reuben by doing this.

I slipped my hand down the front of my pants and over my damp pussy and throbbing clit.

"Are you wet?" Reuben asked.

"Very wet," I whispered. I traced circles around my clit with my fingertips before sliding my fingers inside myself.

"Fuck," Reuben said breathlessly. "Does that feel good?"

"So good," I murmured. I hesitated for a moment before I hooked my thumb around the waistband of my pants and pushed them down, exposing my pussy to him.

"Good girl," he whispered. "You have the most beautiful pussy I've ever seen."

I worked myself slowly, driving my fingers in deeper while I rubbed the heel of my hand against my clit. I slipped the other hand up the front of my singlet to roll my remaining nipple between my thumb and forefinger.

"That's my girl." He hadn't moved, but I saw his arousal tenting the front of his pants, his cock straining against the seams. He didn't touch me or himself, just watched while I drew closer and closer to coming.

"Reuben," I whispered. "I'm going to come."

"Good girl," he said again. "Let me see you come."

I moaned and drove my hand faster and faster before I came in a rush of sensation I hadn't felt in so long. It wasn't the most violent or intense orgasm I ever had. Instead, it was a gentle sweep of pleasure that curled my toes and made me cry out loud.

I slumped back against the pillows and pulled my fingers out of my wetness.

"You're even more beautiful when you come," he said. "So perfect."

Without thinking, I pulled my pyjama pants back up into place and rolled onto my knees. Slowly, and with my eyes still on his, I crawled towards him. I pressed my fingers, still wet with my juices, against his lower lip.

His eyes widened slightly, but he opened his mouth and took my fingers between his lips to suck them clean.

"You even taste perfect," he said as he slid his mouth along the back of my hand. "One day I'm going to taste your pussy for myself." He took my hand in his and kissed the centre of my palm.

"Thank you," I said. I seemed to have said that a lot

in the last couple of weeks. "Thank you for reminding me I'm not his prisoner anymore. I can still live my life in spite of what happened. All of my life." Someday I could let him inside me. I wanted that, when the time came.

"I'm the one who should be thanking you," Reuben said. "Watching you come was a gift. One I won't forget. This first time between us will always be special." He didn't have to say it wouldn't be the last time, that was heavy in the air between us.

"Gianni—" I started softly.

"Also wants to be with you," he finished for me. "I'm well aware. I'm man enough to admit there are things I can't give you that he can. Damon too. As long as you don't choose them instead of me, then I don't see why we can't explore all our options. We want the same thing, what's best for you. That's the only thing that matters." He kissed my forehead and stood to adjust his pants.

"I hope you sleep well." Quiet as a ghost, he slipped back out the door and closed it behind him.

I lay down and drew the blankets over myself. I closed my eyes and did something I hadn't done in a long, long time. I fell into a deep sleep.

———

Reuben

• • •

I stepped away from Mina's room, grimacing at the steel in my pants. I couldn't remember being harder in my life. Watching her touch herself like that, was the single, most erotic sight I'd ever seen. I wanted to touch her. To fuck her. I would, when the time came. Seeing her get off, that was enough. For now.

I opened the door to my room at the back of the house, and stepped inside. I closed the door behind me, but didn't lock it.

If anyone entered my room, they had my permission to be inside my house. No one got past the security system. If they did, they wouldn't get past Gianni and Damon. Both knew better than to come into my private space anyway. Terry wouldn't bother.

That left Mina. She was welcome at any time, regardless of the hour, or if I was sleeping. She was one of very few people who'd survive the experience if she woke me up.

I stepped out of my clothes and left them in a neat pile on the floor. Terry would slip in and take them for washing in the morning.

My bedroom was the largest in the house, the most opulently decorated. It was also the one that looked the least lived-in. I only spent several hours a day here, mostly sleeping. There was no need to step through the door, otherwise. My library was my sanctuary and my office was for working. This was just a place to rest and store my clothes. And wash.

It was to the bathroom I headed. I closed the door behind me and turned on the shower, hot almost to the point of scalding. I stepped onto the black and white penny tiles, the same as in the house's other bathrooms, and under the water.

Washing took only a couple of minutes, but I didn't start on that yet. Instead, I leaned against the walls, the subway tiles cold against my back, and wrapped my hand around my thick cock. My erection under the water, I started to slide my hand up and down, from head to heavy balls.

My eyes closed, I pictured Mina, her legs spread to display her glorious pussy. Her hand moved over her clit, fingers pressed deep inside her. The more she worked herself, the more her fingers glistened with her own juices.

I pumped harder, remembering the way her breath came in pants and tiny moans. I didn't think she was aware of the sounds she made, but I committed each one to memory, seared into my mind like a brand.

I leaned my head back and pressed my eyes shut tighter. My lips curled back in a grimace as my orgasm rose so fast I couldn't stop it. It washed over me with the water, flooding my senses and forcing me to grit my teeth to keep from shouting out loud.

I didn't shout, ever, but I could have screamed her name in that moment. All I could think of was her. When cum exploded out of me in a rush, I wanted to spill myself into her body. I wanted to fill her so full she overflowed. I wanted to hear her scream my name as I pounded into her.

Puffing lightly, I sagged forward, my orgasm fading and leaving me exhausted and not completely satisfied.

I wouldn't be until I came inside her.

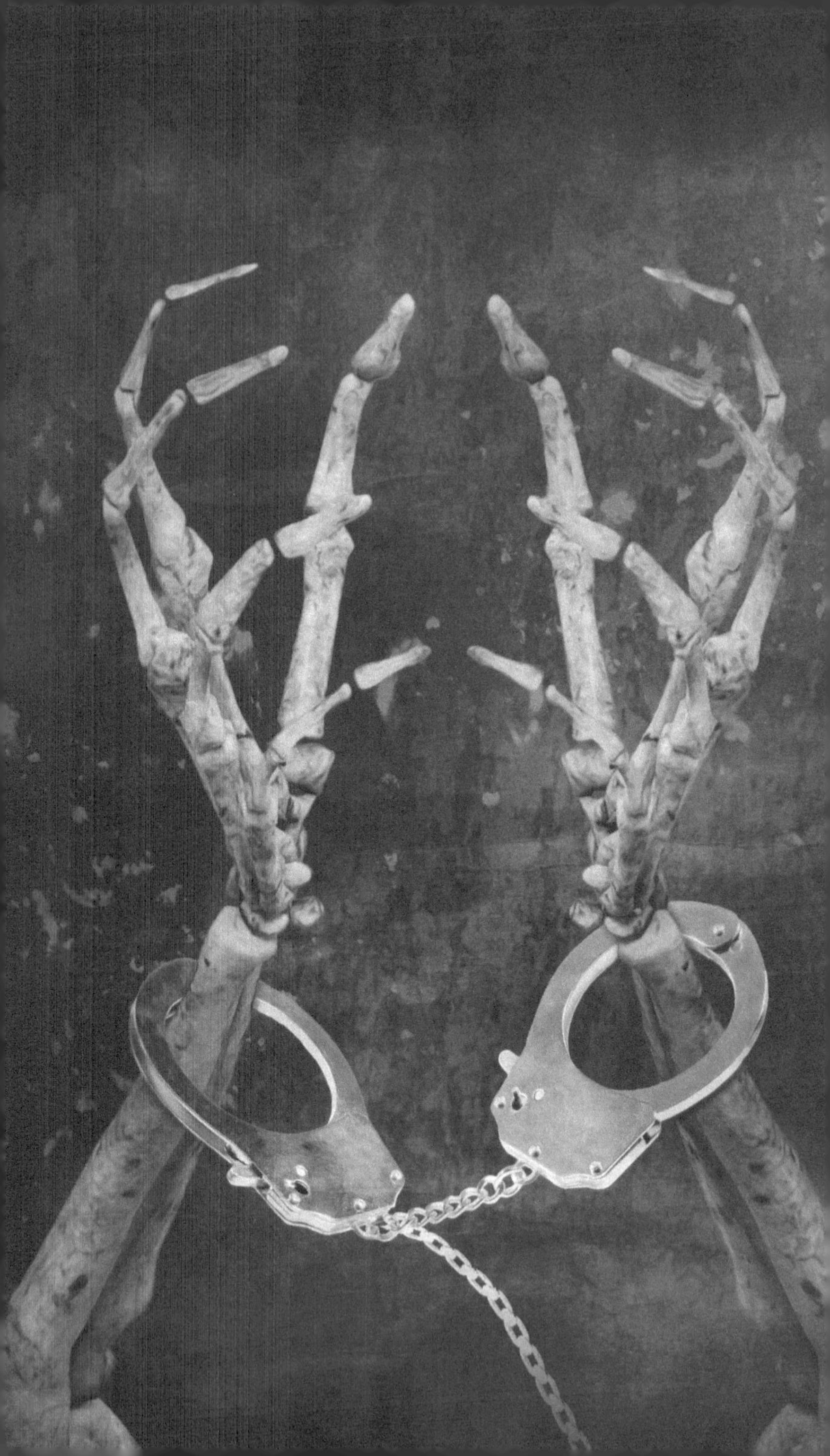

CHAPTER 14

MINA

"I am going to break his scrawny little neck." A female voice came from the kitchen. Not one I recognised.

"You're going to need to get in line," Gianni replied easily. "Your dear brother, Kurt, got himself onto a whole lot of shit lists. Especially mine."

"Fuck that," she said. "If I catch up to him first, he's fucking toast."

"I want him alive." That was Reuben's soft tone.

"So we can kill him slowly and painfully," Gianni added. He sounded very much like he was looking forward to it.

"You might as well go in." Damon spoke behind me, making me startle violently. He gave me a glance before walking past and into the kitchen. Not laughing at me, nor apologetic. He didn't seem to care one way or another if I stayed out in the corridor or joined the conversation.

I was torn between wanting to keep my presence a secret and needing to see Daisy Lasalle for myself.

With the full knowledge my cousin Ric might also be present, I stepped into the kitchen.

Several people sat at the table, including Reuben. Gianni leaned against the island, a coffee mug in his hand with the logo of the Dusk Bay Demons ice hockey team on the side. From what I understood, Reuben's brother Caleb owned the team. Not because he cared about hockey, it was another front for the family.

Everyone turned to look at me as I entered the room. Ric looked at me with surprise, but it was Daisy who caught and held my eyes. She looked enough like her brother to give me chills, but she had the empathy he completely lacked.

She rose from her seat and came to put her arms around me. "If I had a clue what he was doing, I would have put a stop to it. You have to believe I never would have let you go through what he put you through. When I catch up to him, I'm going to kick his sorry ass."

I froze when she touched me, but gradually managed to relax enough to quickly hug her back before I pulled away again.

"I believe you." She wouldn't be here if Reuben didn't think she was sincere. Unless this was some kind of test. Presumably she passed or he wouldn't have allowed her anywhere near me.

"This is a surprise." Ric also stood, but made no move to step towards me. "You grew up, cousin."

"So did you." I wasn't close to him or his brother, but I'd seen him often enough to notice the difference. Only a couple of years older than me, he was barely more than a teenager himself the last time we met.

"Reuben tells me you don't want the rest of the family to know you're here," Ric said. Judging by the expression on his face, he was told something along the lines of, 'tell anyone and you're dead.'

I glanced over to Reuben, who watched everything with his usual measured interest.

"That's right," I said softly. "I'll tell them everything when I'm ready." I couldn't put it off forever, but I could put it off for now.

"They won't hear it from us," Daisy said. "Right, Ric?"

He sat back down and gave her an affectionate smile. "Daze already told me she'd kick me so hard in the balls they'd retreat back up into my body and stay there. Since I'm attached to their current location, I'll keep my mouth shut."

Daisy grinned. "I didn't actually need to threaten him. He already knows what I would have done." She sat back down beside him.

I slipped into a chair beside Reuben and nodded my thanks to Terry who placed coffee in front of me. "I heard you talking about Kurt."

The mood of the kitchen dipped.

"I had no idea the extent of the shit he was up to," Ric said. "As you know, I've been tracking missing shipments for a while now, but haven't been able to pin down who was behind them. I came to the conclusion it was an inside job, but he was good at covering his tracks. Now we know where to look, it should be a lot easier. So far, I've uncovered at least a dozen redirected shipments of gems spanning the last two to three years. Some of those were believed to be intercepted by the cops."

"You think he was behind all of that?" Damon asked. He stood with his shoulder against the wall, legs crossed at his ankles.

Ric looked up at him. "Some of it. A couple of those shipments were stolen on the way to the police lock-up. Others, I suspect never made it into police hands. We were told what happened, but clearly that was a load of bullshit."

"You looked into it?" Reuben asked.

Ric's gaze swivelled to him. "On your orders or those of Caleb, we did. Kurt and anyone working with him was considered a trusted source at the time. This happens once or twice and you can blame outside sources, but after a while it became obvious someone working with us was working against us."

He let out a frustrated breath and shook his head. "If we'd figured it out sooner..." He shot me an apologetic look.

"Kurt was smart enough to spread out these redirections," Damon said. "At least, at the beginning."

"He got cocky," Daisy said. "He got away with it

enough times to think he could keep doing that. He must have realised it wouldn't go unnoticed."

"It's likely he got desperate," Damon said. "He knew, or at least *sensed*, that Ric was onto him. It was only a matter of time before we figured it all out. And we did. He was probably as active as he dared to be, in preparation for fucking off and hiding."

"So he could be anywhere in the world," I said. "With enough money to hide for the rest of his life."

"He could hide for the rest of his life from honest people," Reuben said. "We have resources they don't have."

"Yeah," Gianni agreed. "And we don't care who we kill to get what we want."

I wasn't convinced it would be that simple. I wished I could believe it would be. Kurt knew exactly what he needed to do to evade all of us. With enough money he could change his identity and his face and never be found.

Reuben placed a hand over one of mine. "We will find him. There's nowhere he can hide that's out of reach."

I turned my hand around and laced my fingers with his. My heart actually fluttered. It had never done that before, not for anyone. I liked that it did it now.

"You can't put everything and everyone on this forever," I said. "Sooner or later, we have to move on from him and what he did."

Gianni chuckled. "When Reuben is determined to

see something through, he will. It would take an army of tanks to stop him."

"There's nothing wrong with being driven," Reuben said.

"I didn't say there was," Gianni said. "Just like there's nothing wrong with fixating on a certain goal. Especially one like this."

"Women like a man who knows what he wants, right Mina?" Daisy smiled at me.

"Yes, they do," I said. I couldn't seem to tear my gaze from Reuben. The more I got to know him, the more he fascinated me. He was a stone cold killer, but he could be so gentle. I'd always found him attractive, but he was so closed, like a heavy door on a bank vault.

Now I realised he wasn't shut off because he was unfeeling, but because he was guarded. He was driven, yes, but he was also committed and loyal. When anyone tried to fuck with him or someone he cared about, he fucked back.

The fact he'd go to such an extent to find Kurt suggested he cared for me more deeply than I suspected. This wasn't just revenge for screwing with the Brantley family. He wanted to give me my own revenge and closure.

"No one else knows Mina is here?" Ric asked.

"Just the twins, Caleb, and everyone in this room," Gianni said. "No one else."

"That's as far as it goes," Reuben growled. "No one

else needs to know. Not until Mina decides they need to." His gaze was also locked on me.

"No one else will hear," Daisy assured us. "We'll keep this all about Kurt stealing from the Brantley family. I think Ric is just curious what your brother Zeke will say when he sees Mina."

"I was thinking more of Asher, but yes," Ric agreed. "He's going to find all of this very…interesting."

"I don't care if he doesn't approve," I said softly. "It's not up to him." Trust my cousin to hit the nail on the head though. Yes, I didn't want my brother to see me looking starved and broken, but I also didn't want him to judge any of the choices I voluntarily made. Including being with Reuben.

"Can I be here when he finds out?" Ric asked. "Ouch." He glanced at Daisy, who jabbed him in the ribs with her elbow. "Don't say you don't want to see that too."

"Of course I do, but it's none of our business." She narrowed her eyes at him.

He responded by rolling his eyes playfully and making a face. It was clear that while she kept him in line, he wasn't intimidated by her. Not too much, anyway. What was her relationship with her other two boyfriends like? I didn't know Gunnar, but I'd met Hilton a couple of times. He seemed like the kind of man not to be crossed if people enjoyed living.

Like everyone else in this room, I supposed.

"Exactly," Reuben said. "Your business is finding

Kurt and figuring out whatever else he was up to." He pressed his lips together. "I want to know if there are any other women hidden away."

The smile faded from Daisy's face. "You think there might be? If there are, I'm going to rip his fucking balls off."

"Did I mention that you need to get in line?" Gianni asked. "We don't know if there are others, but if he did this to Mina, he might just as easily have done it to someone else."

Reuben squeezed my hand. It wasn't until then I realised I was trembling. The idea of some other woman locked away, terrified, hungry, used and scarred, it got to me every time the subject came up.

So far, we hadn't found anyone, but that didn't mean they didn't exist. Even worse was the idea that Kurt ran, leaving them to die alone, not found until it was too late. That could so easily have happened to me. If they hadn't found me when they did, I'd be dead in that filthy cage. I might not have been discovered for years.

"I'm so sorry," Daisy whispered. "If there's ever anything I can do, please ask. I can't get my head around my own brother doing this to anyone. I knew he was an asshole, but I didn't know he was a monster." She sounded devastated. Furious.

"It's not your fault," I whispered back. "You're not responsible for what your brother did. He decided to be who he was. Not you or anyone else." Although my father gave him the opportunity. He was as guilty as Kurt, but Daisy wasn't.

"I know, I just feel like I should have seen it," she said. "Maybe there were signs and I missed them."

"We all missed the signs he was up to shady shit," Ric said. "Until we figured it out and got Mina out of there."

"We?" Gianni asked.

Ric shrugged. "I was the one who told you he was up to something. If I hadn't, my cousin wouldn't have been found. So yeah, *we*."

"Touché." Gianni smirked. "You're a DiMarco all right."

Ric grinned. "We're all known for our awesomeness, right Mina?"

I wasn't sure about that, but I managed a small smile in return. "Absolutely. We're amazing."

"You definitely are," Gianni said. "More than amazing."

I wished I felt that way about myself, but it felt good to spend a little time with family. A little piece of normal would go a long way towards helping me heal.

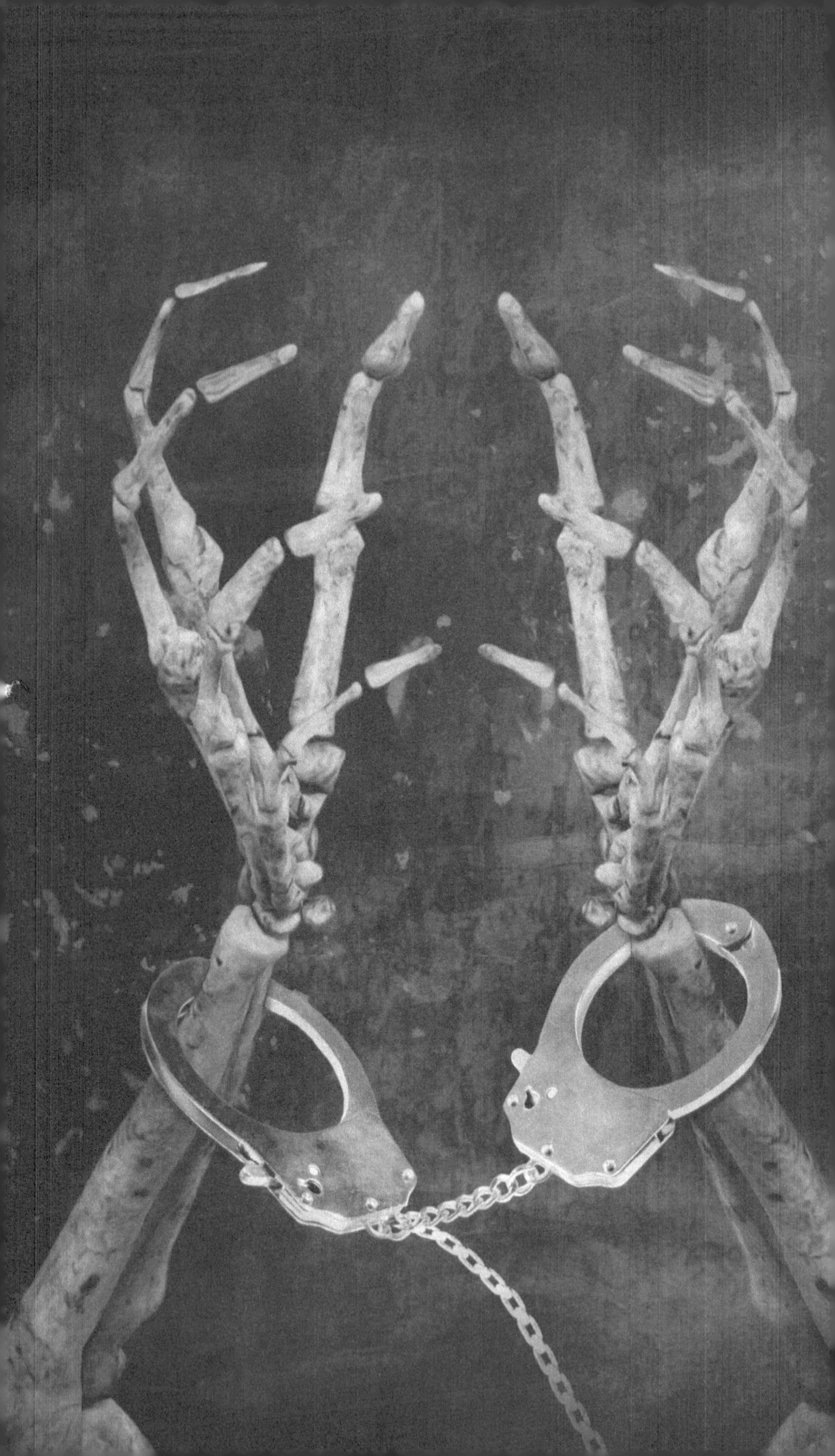

CHAPTER 15

MINA

"You can tell me to fuck off if you want to," Daisy said. She followed me out into the back garden, leaving Ric inside to talk to the other men. "I just thought you might like to have another woman to talk to. Men can be so testosterone-y sometimes."

I glanced over to the vegetable garden where Terry was tending to the plants, clearly not paying any attention to us.

Feet bare, I walked across the neat lawn to the back of the garden where the roses grew. Amongst the trees and fragrant bushes were a pair of stone benches.

I lowered myself down onto one of them. "Yes, they can. I appreciate it, but if you came to apologise again for—" She'd done enough of that as far as I was concerned.

There was nothing to forgive her for, therefore no need to keep saying sorry.

She sat on the other bench. "No. I mean, I won't now. You looked like you could use a friend. Someone who understands what this crazy life is like." She plucked a half-dead rose off one of the bushes and started to pull off the petals and scatter them on the ground.

"I tried to get away from all of this. To live a normal life away from crime, violence and death. Turns out, I kinda like those things." She glanced over at me and grinned. "The moment I saw Ric again, I was done for. I think I was in denial for all those years."

"So you went back," I said. I never considered walking away. I didn't know anyone who had done it successfully, unless you counted my brother, Asher. He seemed to be living his best life away from the craziness.

"I didn't just go back, I brought my daughter with me," she said. "Ric's daughter. I wanted to keep her out of it, but it's in her blood as much as it is in mine. I'm guessing it's in yours too."

I wondered how much she knew about me. Probably not everything. If she did, she probably wouldn't ask me that question.

"I can't imagine living any other way." I watched the petals drop from her hand and flutter to the ground. "I killed a woman the other day." I told Daisy about her.

She nodded and dropped another couple of petals. "Good for you. No one messes with women like us." She closed her hand over the last few petals. "I'm—"

"Don't say sorry," I interrupted. "You're absolutely

right. No one will ever mess with me again. They'd have to kill me first."

"I wouldn't envy them if they did that. Reuben would rip them apart. I saw the way he looks at you. Like he'd go to the centre of hell for you. I've never seen him look at anyone like that. If I'm honest, I'd say I didn't think he was capable of those kinds of emotions. Men like him are— I don't know, they don't like being vulnerable." She opened her hand, turned it around and let the rest of the squashed flower fall to the grass.

"You think caring about someone makes him vulnerable?" I asked.

She glanced over and laughed once. "No, I don't. I just think that's how they see it. That if a big, bad man gives his heart to anyone, they might break it. All of my guys would have thought exactly that. Turns out, loving people makes us stronger and braver. And they get the added bonus of being with me." She grinned.

It was hard not to like her. She was strong and outspoken without needing to be nasty. Ric clearly adored her and the feeling was obviously mutual.

She was right, I needed another woman to talk to. Reuben and Gianni were attentive, but after last night things were different. Reuben and I went past friendship. Whatever this was between us, we couldn't go back to that.

With Daisy, there was no such expectation. We could talk and share things we wouldn't share with any man. Experiences women had that men didn't. Fears and vulnerabilities. The need for constant vigilance against attacks from men like Kurt.

The fact she hadn't seen me in that cage, ragged and filthy, went some way to making me feel more comfortable with her. The woman sitting here now was the only one she'd seen, otherwise she might look at me with more pity than she had. Of all the things I might want from her, pity wasn't one of them.

"I'm not sure if giving his heart to me is something Reuben plans on doing," I said.

She laughed again. "Whether or not he planned it, you already have it. I'm guessing he hasn't said anything, but it's obvious to anyone watching. He's head over heels for you."

She shook her head. "I wouldn't have believed it if I hadn't seen it with my own eyes. Reuben Brantley madly in love with Mina DiMarco. It's like something out of a romance novel."

Was he madly in love? It seemed like a stretch. Caring about someone and being in love weren't always the same thing.

"Gianni looks at you the same way," Daisy added. "Damon keeps his cards close to his chest, but it wouldn't surprise me if you four ended up like me and my guys."

"They're just protective," I said. "And pissed off at Kurt for stealing from them. That's all it is."

She stared at me in a way that was disturbingly like her brother. "That's not all it is. They care for you very much. I know after what you've been through, you're not ready to rush into anything. I saw that they know that too, or they'd be wearing their balls as necklaces right now. Before I leave, I'll give you my details. If they ever overstep, you're welcome to contact me and I'll fly up and deal with them." She seemed completely sincere.

"Did I mention I killed a woman?" I asked flatly.

She grinned. "So you did. I'm sure you're capable of making them eat their own nuts, but if you need help, I'm here for you. So is Ric. He'd be hating himself right now for what happened to you. We trusted Kurt and his associates and we shouldn't have."

"You should be able to trust your brother," I said. I trusted both of mine, more or less.

Okay, I trusted Asher. Dane tended to look out for his own ass. He used to, anyway. Maybe he'd changed. Maybe he hadn't.

"If Ric hadn't looked into things, I wouldn't be here. I'm grateful to him."

"Still, it's his job to make sure shit like this doesn't happen. Caleb was pissed at him. If there's anything Caleb doesn't like, it's losing money. Reuben doesn't like it either, but Caleb is worse. I think it comes with being the second oldest brother. He always has to prove himself. Or maybe he just has a really small cock." She grinned.

I actually let out a small, choking laugh at that. "I

suppose that's possible. I guess I should be grateful to Caleb too, for pushing Ric to keep looking."

"Do yourself a favour and never tell Caleb that," Daisy said. "If he thinks you owe him something, he'll hold that over you. He'll want something in return. Whatever that something is, it's bound to be a thing you don't want to give."

I recoiled. "He wouldn't want—"

She grimaced. "No, not sex. Who knows what it would be, but he wouldn't be stupid enough to try that with someone Reuben is interested in. He'd be too scared Reuben would take all his power away from him. Which is exactly what Reuben *would* do. No, Caleb would ask for something else. It's best you don't let him put you in that position. Trust me, I worked for Caleb for years. I see him all the time. He's always got an angle he's working. And he wants to use everyone around him to his own advantage."

"That doesn't sound different to anyone else in my life," I said. "Everyone wants something." Which led me to wonder what she wanted.

"Ain't that the truth," she said with a laugh. "Some of us just want what's best for you. Including me. I can't even imagine the things you've gone through. Hearing about it was enough to make me want to puke." Her smile had faded to an expression of regret.

"You must be a lot stronger than me, because there's no way I'd survive five minutes down there, much less five years."

"You might have found a way out," I said. I'd tried more times than I could count but failed and eventually gave up. In the end, the only hope I had was for death. Even that seemed like too much to wish for.

Daisy fixed me with a firm look. "If there was a way out of there, you would have found it. I know Kurt, he wouldn't have left even the smallest opportunity. He was always like that. He thought everything through, every scenario, every possibility. That was exactly why he got past us for so long. He's intelligent and meticulous. I'm coming to realise he might be a sociopath. The point is, not being able to get away from him is not a reflection on you or your abilities. You did what so many other people wouldn't be able to do. You survived and walked away. I don't think you have any idea how incredible that really is."

"I just…" I didn't know how to respond to that. All I did was take it one minute at a time. Count the bars around me and the lines on the ceiling. Survive when Kurt came to give me what meagre food he bothered to drop into the cage. Switch off as best I could when he used my body. Was that really so incredible?

"I did what I had to do," I said finally. "I switched off my feelings and focused on breathing and not what was happening around me. I listened to my heartbeat and counted them to calm myself. I took myself out of there, in my head." I curled and flexed the fingers of one hand as I spoke.

Daisy gave me a searching look, but nodded. "See

what I mean? You're stronger than you think you are. Switching off the world around you and focusing on one thing is difficult to do without practice."

In that moment, I felt like she could see right through me. Like she fully understood me and all my darkest secrets.

I lifted my chin. That was all. Not a word of warning, no threats. Just a short, silent motion.

She lowered hers. She understood and wouldn't say anything to anyone. This was between us and us alone.

"My friends call me Daze." She held out a hand to me.

I took it without hesitation and squeezed before letting it go again. "Mine used to call me Mina Sunshine, but now I'm just Mina." I used to go by another name, but we wouldn't talk about that. Not now. Maybe not ever.

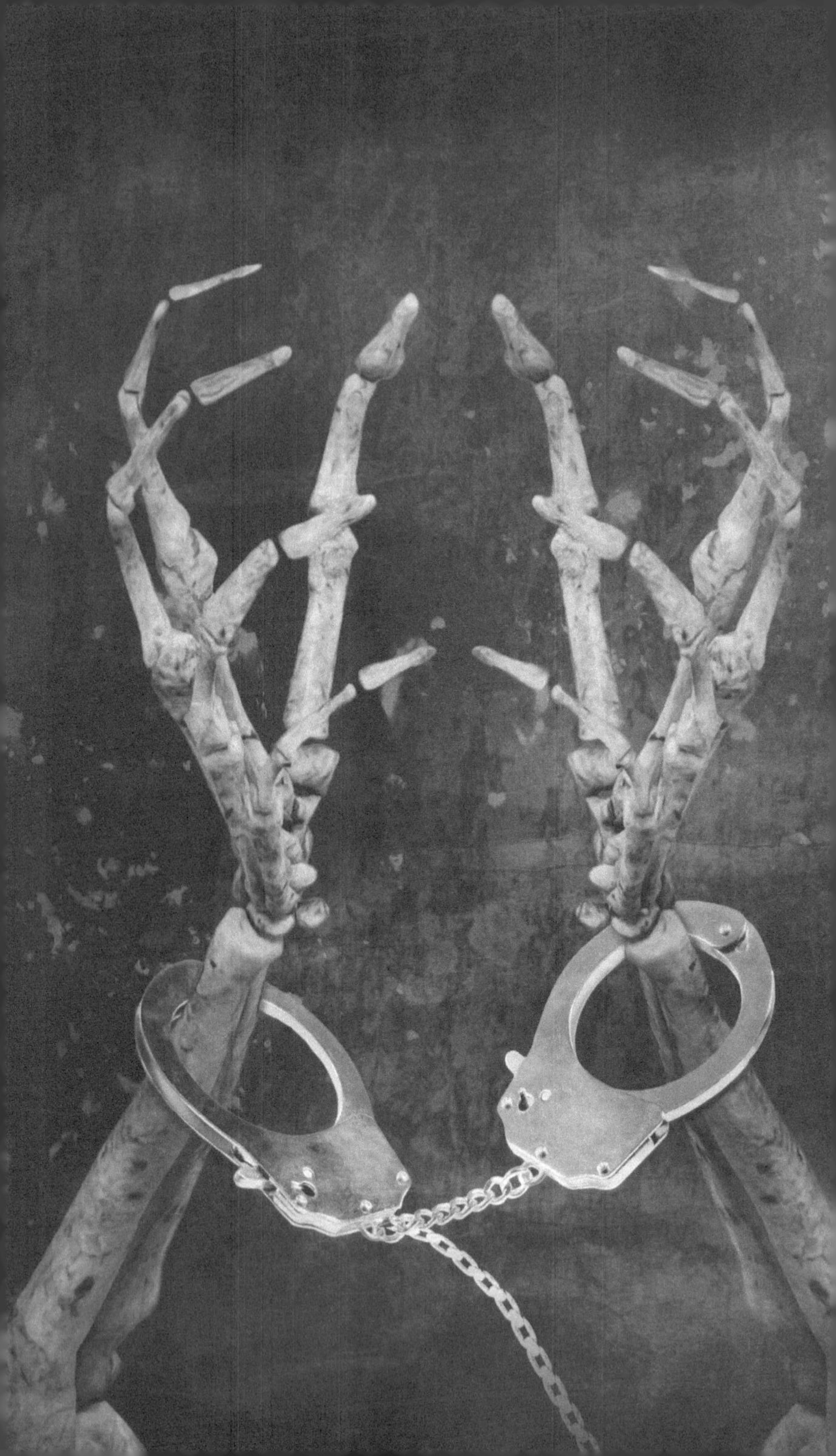

CHAPTER 16

MINA

"I have a surprise for you," Gianni said. "I was thinking about the way you sliced that woman open the other day."

He picked up the plates from lunch, took them into the kitchen and gestured for me to follow him outside.

"Don't damage the roses," Damon called out after us. "Terry will be pissed."

Terry grunted his agreement and continued to slice potatoes to throw into a pot. The knife in his hand was huge and, judging by the way the blade sliced effortlessly through the potato skin, sharp.

"*I'll* be pissed," Reuben said as he finished his coffee.

"No roses will be harmed in the making of this surprise," Gianni said. He rolled his eyes at them playfully and closed the door behind us.

"What about the woman?" I asked.

He hadn't brought me a group of people to practice on. That was probably for the best. Instead, a couple of large targets were set up in the centre of the lawn.

"It's less about her and more about using a knife." He picked up a box from beside the door and opened it. Inside, several small knives lay on black velvet. Sun glinted off the steel like a wink, or a challenge.

"You want me to throw those?" I guessed.

"I think knife throwing is a skill every girl should have." He picked up a knife and set the box back down. "Have you done this before?"

I opened and closed my mouth.

He pressed the heel of his hand to his forehead. "Of course you haven't done it *recently*. I'm such a fucking donkey sometimes."

I snorted a laugh. "You're not a donkey. I have done it, but like you said, not recently. I'm probably rusty as hell." I leaned down to pick up another of the knives. Picturing the blade right in the centre of Kurt's forehead made me smile.

"This is going to be torture on my dick," Gianni murmured. "Okay, watch me and that might help it come back to you. If not, there's plenty of time to practice."

He turned to face the target, aimed and sent the knife flying from his hand. It landed just to the right of the centre of the target.

"Apparently I need to practice more too." He shrugged. Even if his aim was slightly off, he still would have killed the person he was aiming at. "You try."

I regarded him for a moment before leaning over to pick up two more knives. I eyed the target, cleared my mind and let the knives loose, one at a time. The first landed dead centre of the target. The second landed to the right of his and the third directly above.

He stared at me, then burst out laughing. "I should have known you'd be good at this. I bet you could hit the target blindfolded."

"I was aiming to put them all in the centre," I said regretfully. "I'm rusty."

"You're fucking amazing and my cock is hard as hell now." The front of his jeans were tented, his expression strained. "I never could resist a woman who knew how to handle a knife."

"Maybe we should stop," I suggested. I admit to being curious to see what was under the denim. He looked so big. My clit pulsed in agreement, but I couldn't tell if my trembling was from fear or desire. Possibly both.

"I definitely think we should keep going," he said. He adjusted the front of his pants and walked to the target to pull the knives free.

He handed me two and kept two for himself before stepping in front of the other target. "Who taught you?" He aimed and hit closer to the centre of the target.

"My sister, Rose," I said. "She's a big believer in women taking care of themselves and each other."

My first knife hit the centre of the target, but the second went too far to the left again. I wouldn't be satisfied until they were both lodged in the same hole.

"I've heard that about her," he said. "She seems almost as badass as you."

I walked over to pull the knives out of the target. "She's much more badass than I ever was."

"You miss her?" He seemed to have forgotten to practice and was standing looking at me, a knife held loosely in his hand.

"I miss her a lot," I said. "Her and Asher. Dane too, I guess. Do you think I should contact them?"

"If you're ready." He remembered the knife and turned to throw it. "No one is going to pressure you into anything. Least of all me. I haven't spoken to my family in years."

This was the first time he mentioned a family. Until now, I hadn't wanted to intrude by asking.

"Why haven't you spoken to them?" I asked.

He rubbed a hand over his chin. "It's a long story. Mostly they're assholes and I'm better off without them." There was clearly more to it than that. I decided not to push. He'd tell me if he was ready.

"Their loss." I threw again, this time getting the blades closer together.

"Very much so." He adjusted his pants again. "What other skills do you have that are hot enough to almost make me come in my pants?"

I walked over and spoke softly in his ear. "I can pick locks."

He groaned. "Fucking hell, woman. You really want to see me make a mess, don't you?"

I laughed softly. "Is this where I say I'm sorry?"

"You can try, but I wouldn't believe it for a moment. You seem to enjoy torturing me." He was grinning as he said it.

I was close enough to reach out and touch the front of his pants with the tips of my fingers lightly. I swallowed at how hard he felt. How big.

"Sweetheart," he said softly. "I won't ask you to—"

"I want to." This was all about me taking back my power. I knew he'd let me go as far as I was comfortable and wouldn't say a word if I pulled back.

I worked the button of his jeans out of the hole and slid down the zipper. I wasn't surprised to find brightly coloured boxers, decorated with cartoon characters. None I recognised, but very Gianni.

I pushed them down to free his massive erection. A piercing glittered in the tip. Three or four more decorated the underside of his cock.

"Jacob's ladder," he said. "For the pleasure of my partner. When she's ready."

Intrigued, I ran the tip of my finger across each of the steel bars and the warm skin between them.

"Did they hurt?"

"Yeah, but I like pain," he replied easily. "Giving and receiving it. Don't worry, I only give it without consent

to people who deserve it. I know how to be restrained."
He swallowed hard, clearly holding back the urge to thrust himself into my hand.

"I thought you might," I ran my finger up and down his length, enjoying the feeling of hot, throbbing pulse beneath thin, blood-darkened skin.

He moaned softly. "Can I ask you something?"

I glanced at his face, then back down to his cock. "That depends what it is."

He chuckled softly. "I guess it would. I'm wondering if you were ever with anyone. By your choice."

I stopped stroking to look back up at him. "No," I whispered. "There was never anyone I wanted to…fuck. None that wanted me, too." None I knew of anyway. It wouldn't have crossed my mind that Reuben might have. He seemed so far out of reach, we might as well have lived in different worlds.

"Anyone who doesn't want you is out of their mind," Gianni said. "But I promise when that happens between us, it will be fully with your consent. No pressure from me. No obligation."

"When?" I ran my whole hand up and down his length before curling my fingers around him.

"When," he said firmly. His eyes half closed. "There will come a day when I slide my cock deep into your sweet pussy. But for now, this is enough." He rolled his hips as I started to slowly pump his cock. "You have magic hands."

"I don't know about that." I watched his face while I

worked him, revelling in how responsive he was. Everything he felt right now was because of me. Because of my touch. Because my hand was wrapped around his cock. I was the one in control. I decided how fast or slow we went.

"I do," he said with a groan. "Fuck, sweetheart, I'm going to… Come." He gave me time to pull away before he gritted his teeth and thrust his hips faster. He slid in and out of my hand until he stilled. Hot, pearly cum squirted out of his tip, onto my fingers like the blood from the woman's neck.

He sagged forward, puffing lightly. "Shit, that was good. Better than good."

I uncurled my hand from him. My fingers were coated with his release, thick and warm.

"You did that to me," he said softly. "Just looking at you makes me want to come. You let me do that and I thank you. No one ever got me off that hard before. I bet your pussy is even better."

My pussy pulsed in response to his touch, his orgasm, my power over his body. I'd never felt anything like it before. I felt more powerful than I had when I killed that woman.

I looked up at him, raised my hand to my mouth and started to lick my fingers clean.

Gianni's eyes widened. "Just when I think you couldn't get any hotter, you fucking do. One day, I'm going to come in your mouth and watch you swallow every drop, but this is almost as good. How do I taste?"

I hadn't reached my pointer finger yet. It was still covered in a thick layer of cum. I lifted it to his mouth and, when he opened for me, pressed my finger inside.

He closed his lips around and sucked. "Mmm, delicious," he said around my fingertip. "I taste good on your skin."

He sucked for a while longer before pulling his mouth back with a wet pop. "This just cements what I already knew. We belong together."

I was starting to think that too. I couldn't deny my attraction to him and Reuben, and my curiosity about Damon, but it went deeper than that. They seemed to understand me in a way no one else had before. They let me be me and take my time to settle back into life outside the cage. No coercion, no pressure, no judgement.

All of those were reasons I wasn't ready to see my family yet. Dane in particular would judge me for being here and probably try to manipulate the situation to benefit him in some way. He'd encourage my relationship with Reuben, but only because he'd hope to gain power for himself from it. He was always the most ambitious in our family. The one most likely to throw the rest of us under a bus if it helped him in some way.

I placed enough pressure on myself to put the past behind me without having someone like him making things more difficult.

"Those look like some deep thoughts," Gianni said. He'd pulled up his pants and fastened them, and was now looking at me like he wasn't sure if he should offer to get me off or not. He clearly wanted to, but would let me take the lead in that too.

"I was just thinking about my family," I said. Before he could respond, I stood on my toes and brushed my lips over his. He tasted of coffee and cum, with a touch of salt. A delicious combination.

He placed a hand on my upper arm and deepened the kiss in a way that let me pull away when I was ready. When his tongue pressed against my lips, I opened them to let him slide inside. Tentatively, I slid my tongue against his.

My body throbbing, I eventually drew back. "I've never been kissed like that before."

He smiled. "Neither have I. Your mouth is even more perfect than your hand."

I laughed softly. I wanted him to touch me more, but not yet. The huge steps I'd already taken were enough for now.

"We should get back to practising," I said. "You might be able to concentrate now."

He chuckled. "With you next to me, never."

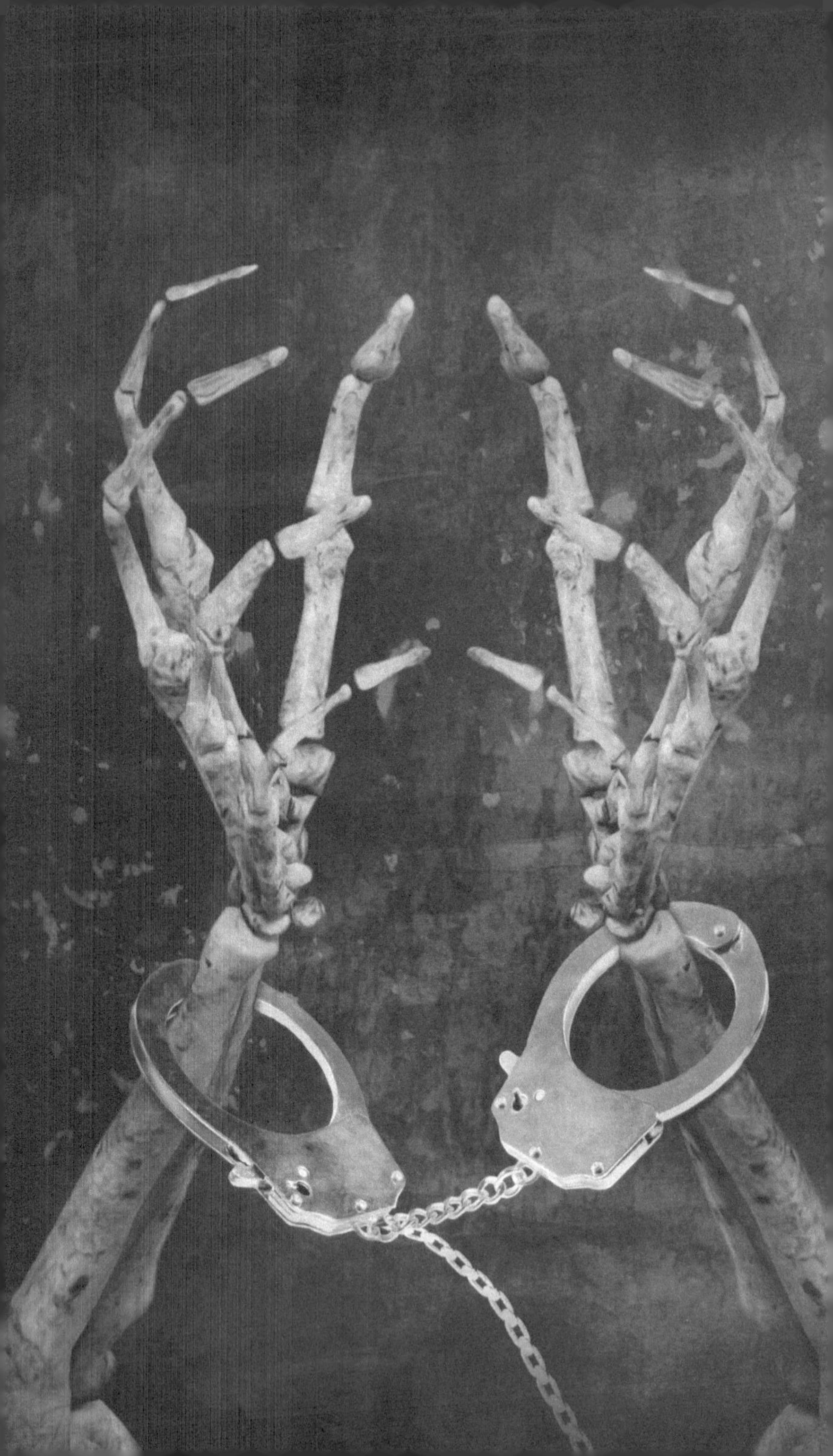

CHAPTER 17

REUBEN

I stepped away from the window as Mina and Gianni resumed practising throwing knives. Her skill didn't surprise me. Watching her hand stroke Gianni's cock did. I'd watched as he thrust and came on her fingers, my cock aching to do the same.

"She's a distraction," Damon said.

I glanced over to him. "Perhaps. That changes nothing. I'm not sending her away."

"I didn't expect you would." He eyed the bulge in my trousers, which I was trying hard to ignore and deflate. I didn't look at his. I didn't need to; I knew it was there. We'd both watched.

"What do you expect then?" I walked past him to place my empty cup in the kitchen.

"I don't know. Since you found her, you've been obsessed with finding Kurt Lasalle. Killing him won't change what he did to her." Damon leaned his hip against the island and crossed his arms.

"It'll make me feel a whole fuck ton better. Knowing he's out there is pissing me off," I growled.

"Me too," he said easily. "I want to make an example of him as much as you do. He spent long enough going behind our back. It's past time he paid for that, regardless of what he did or didn't do to Mina."

I wanted to tell him he had his priorities backwards, but the point wasn't relevant right now. The fact was, Lasalle operated behind our backs and we needed to send a message that it wouldn't be tolerated.

"This is personal," I stated. "You feel responsible for not seeing what he was doing sooner."

Damon took pride in keeping a tight leash on our businesses. And on the people who worked for me. If they put a foot out of line, he was the one who either pulled them back, or cut it off. Often literally. This level of betrayal was something else.

His expression suggested I was exactly right. He looked ready to grind his teeth.

"I should have seen it. Ric and Caleb didn't, but I fucking *should* have. You're right it's fucking personal. That prick must have been laughing at us while he was trying to build an empire to rival the Brantley family."

He curled his hands into fists.

"Should I punish you for missing it?" I asked, my own tone deadpan as ever. "I could have Gianni remove a few of your toenails. It's not his usual method, but I'm sure he'd make an exception for you. Or he could lock you in a room and play some of his music at full volume for an hour or two."

That sounded like torture to me.

"You probably should punish me," Damon grumbled. He exhaled out his nose in frustration. "I fucked up. Since when do you tolerate failure?"

"Since I need you to find him," I said. "You have skills and contacts. The moment he pops up, you'll know." Damon's network was enviable. With my money and backing, he'd grown it into something both impressive and valuable. His network, and him, were assets I wasn't going to let go, whatever the cost.

"Which is exactly why I'm pissed off: I didn't know what he was up to. All those contacts and skills and the fucker still got past me." He ran a hand over the back of his hair. "What the fuck did I miss? I've gone over everything for the last three or four years and there's nothing. Not one thing to indicate what he was up to."

"He was a sneaky prick," I said. "Smart enough to pull it off and low-key enough to stay under the radar."

"I should have been smarter," Damon insisted. "If he got away with shit, fuck only knows who else is out there getting away with other things."

"We've increased our eyes and ears," I said. "Nothing else is getting past any of us. You said word is already out on the street about what happened in the ice cream parlour?"

Damon dropped his hand against thigh, a sure sign he was winning against his annoyance.

"It has. It's set a few people on edge. Anyone twitchy, I've put extra people on them. If they have a reason to be twitchy, we'll find it. I've also found two more fronts for Kurt's businesses. One was a pet shop. The other was a pub."

"Hiding behind the pussies," I remarked.

Damon chuckled. "If I didn't know better, I'd think Gianni is rubbing off on you."

My mind was immediately back on Mina, rubbing him. My cock twitched in response. Ached to feel her hand on me. Stroking, caressing, coaxing.

I cleared my throat. "Just making an observation. You dealt with both premises?"

"Most of the staff were oblivious," Damon said. "The ones believed to be working for him are being followed. People are watching both establishments. If Kurt turns up at either of them, we'll know. Hopefully he'll get thirsty at some point soon."

We both knew he wouldn't turn up anywhere so obvious, especially if he did the smart thing and left the country. This wasn't a complete waste of time. Reminding people they wouldn't get away with trying to fuck me over was worth the effort.

I nodded. "Good work. We could use someone who's ready to turn on him. Someone who knows enough about him but is willing to spill everything for the right price."

"There must be someone out there like that," Damon agreed. "I've been looking, but so far nothing. If Kurt trusted anyone to that extent, they're hiding as well as he is. He didn't even trust his sister enough to fill her in."

"Good, because Daisy Lasalle working with him would be fatal to her," I said. Not to mention devastating for us. I much preferred to have her on our side, than working against us. Especially given that she and Mina seemed to have formed a friendship. I'd allow that to continue for Mina's sake.

"One thing I have been able to ascertain," Damon said. "Whatever Kurt was up to, he didn't seem to be working with Samuel Bell. If anything, we may have a mutual enemy in the prick."

"He stole from Bell too?" I shouldn't have been surprised by that. Someone like Kurt would have known to spread out his movements. It was unlikely Samuel Bell and I would compare notes, and put two different events together.

Damon shrugged. "At this point, it's hearsay. It's unlikely we'll get the truth from the Bell family, but a contact of a contact spoke about several missing shipments over the last few years. It could have been Lasalle or it could have been someone else. It wasn't us. Not unless the twins are getting up to things you didn't endorse."

"I wouldn't put it past them," I said. I wouldn't be pleased if they went behind my back, but stealing from the enemy wasn't something I gave a shit about, endorsed or not. I had no sympathy for any member of the Bell family. Animosity yes, in abundance, but not sympathy.

"Do you ever worry those two will get out of control, boss?" Damon asked.

"That question assumes they were in control to start with," I said dryly. "No, I don't. They have their moments, but I don't question their loyalty. No more than I question yours. Or Gianni's. They're outrageous sometimes, but they have the family interests at heart."

I'd never tell anyone how fond I was of Hunter and Parker. They probably wouldn't believe it anyway. I was, after all, the coldhearted prick who headed the family. Incapable of emotion, even anger.

I felt all of that and more, I just hid it better than most.

"Should I worry they might come after my job?" Damon asked, looking completely unworried.

"Without a doubt," I replied, with no inflection. "I didn't say they weren't ambitious. They're probably plotting how to take my job as well as yours."

"They better not," Damon growled. "Unless you plan to retire someday."

Before Mina, I would have scoffed at that suggestion. I wasn't even forty and the family business was my whole life.

Now, I found myself with different priorities. Priorities I never expected to have. The women I was involved with in the past were nothing but brief flings. A fuck or two to release tension. Usually, they worked for me and knew I wasn't looking for anything more. I always made that extremely clear.

Mina changed all of that. Around her, I could be someone more than Reuben Brantley, mob boss. I could admit I had feelings I'd put aside for so long I was surprised to find I still had them. They hadn't withered away and died from lack of use. No, they'd lain dormant until the moment I saw her face again.

In that second I understood I'd put them aside to wait for her. She was it for me. She had been for the longest time. I had no idea when I'd fallen for her, but I had and there was no going back.

That realisation made me even more determined to find Lasalle and fuck him up. He'd pay for all the years he kept me from her. He'd pay fucking dearly.

"Someday," I echoed. "Not any day soon, but eventually. I might retire to that nice cottage beside the forest where I can put my feet up in front of a fire and read a book."

"Three days," Damon said.

I frowned questioningly at him. "Three days?"

"Yes. That's my guess on how long it'd take before you got bored and wanted to get back to work." He actually looked slightly amused, which for him was the equivalent of hysterical laughter.

I smirked. "Give me some credit. It would be four and a half days minimum. Maybe four and three quarters." Then I'd be looking for gems to traffic, politicians to bribe and ways to make even more money. I was addicted to power almost to the extent as I was addicted to Mina.

No, I didn't want help to recover from either of those addictions.

"Maybe even five," Damon said. "I guess you won't be going anywhere anytime soon then."

"Probably not," I agreed. Realistically, men in my position rarely lived long enough to retire. There was always someone plotting my death. Someday they might even succeed.

As if he read my mind, Damon said, "I'll do my best to make sure you live long enough to change your mind. Reading in front of a fire sounds relaxing. Not as much fun as fucking in front of one."

"I can always do one, then the other," I said. "That would keep me from being bored."

Now I was thinking about Mina's pussy and the way it glistened with her juices as she touched herself. I wanted to slide my cock into her so much it hurt. I'd waited this long, I could be patient for a while longer. No matter how much it hurt. Having blue balls was better than losing her forever by forcing her to do something she wasn't ready for. That would be unforgivable.

"I'm sure you—"

Whatever Damon was going to say, his phone ringing interrupted him. Not with an Abbie Hart song as his ringtone. Not Wolf Venom either, thank fuck.

He pulled his phone out of his pocket and pressed the screen before putting it to his ear. While he listened to the person on the other end, he frowned, deeper and deeper.

"Shit."

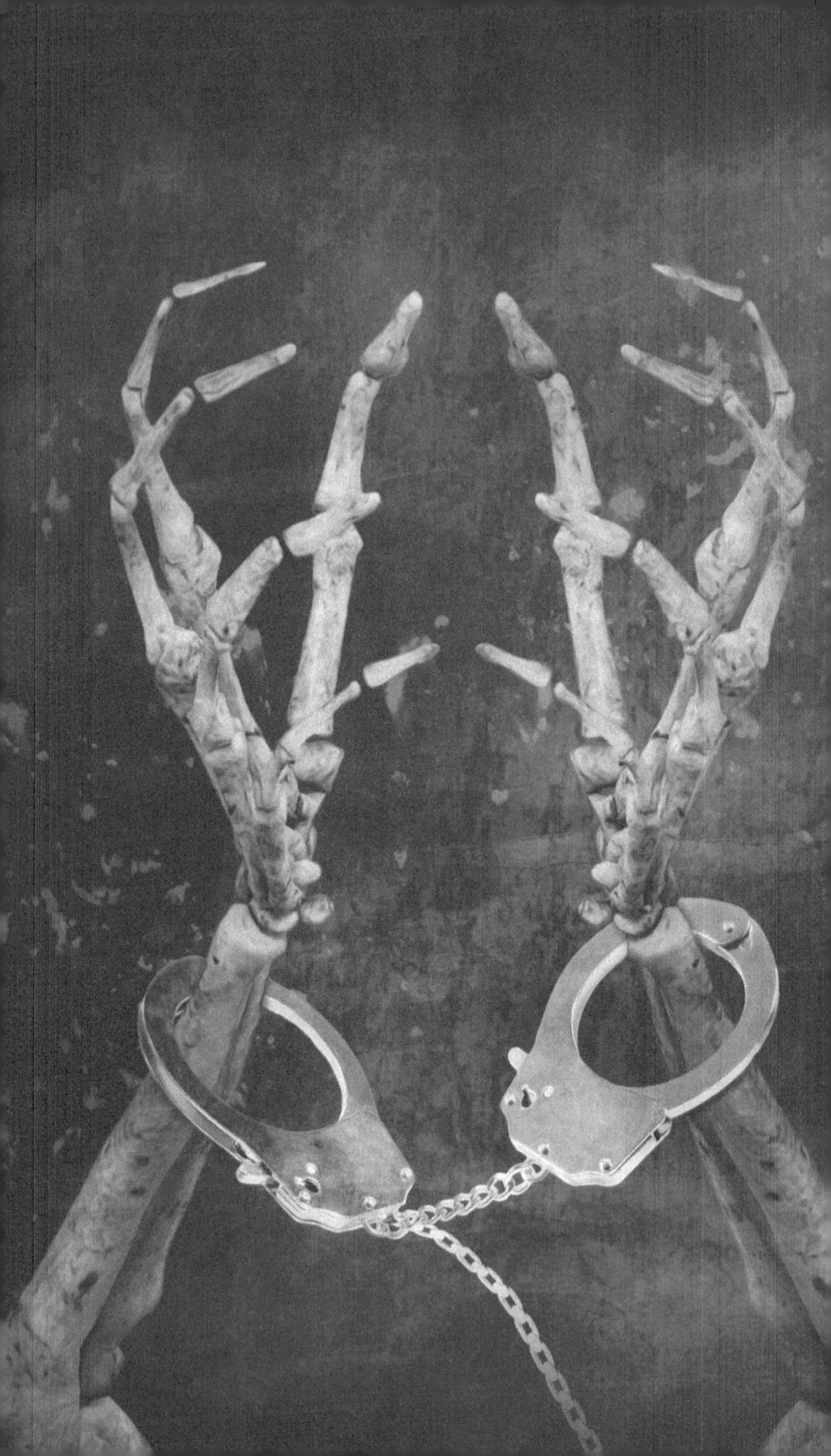

CHAPTER 18

MINA

"Shit."

I followed Gianni into the kitchen in time to hear Damon on the phone. He looked pissed off. The moment he noticed me standing near the door, his expression closed down tight. He ended the call and lowered the phone from his ear.

"What is it?" Gianni asked. "Don't tell me they've sold out of your favourite brand of chocolate again?"

Damon gave him a look that would have withered anyone, but Gianni grinned.

"He's a real bitch when he doesn't get his chocolate," he whispered loudly.

"Fuck off," Damon told him. He glanced at Reuben, then at me.

"If it's about Kurt, she should hear it," Reuben said.

"I'm not sure if it is," Damon said. He rubbed a hand over the back of his neck. "Someone matching his description just flew into Sydney from Hong Kong. It could be him or he could be completely unrelated."

A chill passed all the way through me. Was the room this cold a moment before? It felt icy right then.

Gianni raised a hand to touch my arm.

I flinched. I hadn't forgotten about Kurt, but I'd packed him into a box in my mind and pushed him aside for the last hour or so.

Now, Damon's words brought everything back in a rush. I knew I'd have to see Kurt in order to kill him, but the idea of being face-to-face with him, looking him in the eyes, him looking back at me with his usual contempt, made my stomach heave.

"It's okay, sweetheart," Gianni said gently. "You don't have to see him."

"It might not be him," Damon said. "The twins followed him to the location about twenty kilometres from here. They're keeping an eye on him. They'll let us know if he leaves."

Reuben nodded. "Get the car ready. We'll see for ourselves." His gaze lingered on me.

"I'm coming with you," I said firmly. "If it's him, I need to know. And if it's not, I want to know that too."

"If it is him, chances are he'll be ready for us," Damon said. Again, he looked at me, eyes unreadable.

"We won't let any harm come to her," Gianni said. "I won't let anything happen to her." He sounded ready to take on an army single-handed. "She can bring a couple of knives."

Reuben pressed his lips together, his blue eyes contemplative. "She can come with us. I'd prefer that to leaving her here."

Damon looked irritated, but turned on the heels of his leather shoes and stalked towards the garage.

"I'm guessing he didn't have his quota of chocolate today," Gianni remarked.

"I've never known him to eat chocolate," Reuben said.

Gianni nodded. "That's exactly my point. If he ate some once in a while, he might lighten up."

"Fuck off," Damon said over his shoulder.

"You know you love me," Gianni called out after him.

Without looking back, Damon flipped him off. He wrenched open the garage door and disappeared inside.

Reuben shook his head slightly and rolled his eyes before following Damon.

"Should you antagonise him like that?" I asked.

"Definitely," Gianni agreed. He made no move to touch me or step closer. "I meant what I said."

"About taking care of me, or about me bringing knives?" I asked.

He smiled. "Yes." He grabbed up the box we'd taken outside and tucked it under his arm. "Unless you'd prefer a gun."

"I can shoot." Of course I could. That was a skill we learned from an early age. Both my parents insisted. My father used to take us to the range to practice regularly. "But I prefer knives." They were easier to hide and quieter to use. Subtle and discreet. Until someone had the blade embedded in their brain.

"I sensed that about you," Gianni said. "I thought to myself, *she doesn't seem like a gun person*. Neither is Reuben. Don't get me wrong, he can shoot a man between the eyes from a distance, but he prefers to leave pulling of the trigger to people like me and Damon. And the twins."

That sounded about right. Why get your hands dirty when someone else could do it for you?

I walked behind Gianni to the garage. "Why do you think he came back?"

"Why does anyone do anything?" He opened the back door of the SUV and gestured for me to climb inside. "Unfinished business or money. People are often motivated by one or the other."

I slid in and he closed the door behind me.

"Or desperation." Damon drove the SUV out onto the streets which were surprisingly quiet for this time of day. Quiet enough to make me shiver again.

"Or for a good cup of coffee," Gianni added. "People can do a shit load of dubious things for one of those. Look at Damon, for example. You know he doesn't do this for the money. Not just for my attention either."

"Give the woman a knife so she can shut you up," Damon growled.

Gianni chuckled. "She'd never use a knife on me.

Well, not unless I ask nicely." He glanced over at me and winked.

In spite of my anxiety at the idea of seeing Kurt again, my heart fluttered. Thinking about his cock, the way he came in my hand, and the kiss we shared, was a better use of my thoughts. A healthier one. I would have liked to focus on that, but Kurt was too dominant over my mind right now. I'd spent five years with him occupying my thoughts. It was a difficult habit to break. Was it impossible? I hoped not.

"Is that something you ask often?" I managed to ask. He'd mentioned enjoying pain, did that include knives and blood?

"Only if my partner is someone I implicitly trust," he said. "I'd prefer not to be stabbed mid-fuck if I can help it. A few nicks and slices, on the other hand…"

"If anyone was going to be stabbed mid-fuck, it would be you," Damon said.

"Are you offering?" Gianni asked.

"To stab you? Definitely." Damon glanced at the rear view mirror.

"He means with his cock," Gianni whispered loudly. "I told you he loves me."

"And I told you to fuck off, but here you are," Damon said.

I leaned forward as far as my seatbelt would allow and said to Reuben, "Are they always like this?"

They reminded me of the playful arguments my brother Asher had with Reuben's brother Zeke. They'd been friends since school, practically brothers. Thick as thieves, my mother used to say. When it came to each other, they had no filter. The nastier the words, the harder they laughed. I'd forgotten about that until now. Listening to them slinging insults back and forth always made me giggle.

He sat around to look back at me. "Probably. I tend to tune them out."

Gianni clutched his heart. "Boss, you wound me."

"You'll live," Reuben told him. He offered me the faintest of smiles.

"He really loves me too," Gianni said, lowering his hand back into his lap. "Obviously he does, or he wouldn't share you with me."

"Don't make me change my mind," Reuben said.

"That's up to Mina," Gianni said.

Reuben turned around further and gave him a look that said otherwise. That I belonged to him and he would decide on my behalf if anyone tried to force his hand.

"Like I said, she's a distraction," Damon said. "You two shouldn't be disagreeing over a woman. With all due respect, boss."

Reuben grunted and turned back around.

If I didn't already have the impression Damon didn't like me, I did after that comment.

Did he expect me to walk away from them both or for them to walk away from me? Maybe he thought they should cut my throat and leave me to die by the side of the road.

I eyed the box of knives. I could snatch a couple of them out there before Gianni could move a muscle. I could slice open his throat while he was still thinking about doing the same to me. His blood could coat my hand the way his cum had, thick and hot. I could watch the light fade from his dark eyes as his life slipped away. I could press my hand against his chest and feel the last of his heartbeats, before he fell still.

My hand twitched.

"If you're a distraction, I'm happy to be distracted," Gianni said softly. He was looking at me with half-lidded eyes, as though completely aware of the thoughts churning in my mind.

Of course he was. He acted silly at times, but it was a cover for the man underneath. He was clever, obser-vant and read people the way Reuben read books. He hadn't lived as long as he had without knowing exactly what was going on with the people around him.

I folded my hands over each other. "I'm not a distraction. I'm just a woman trying to reclaim her life from a fucking monster."

I kept my voice low, but loud enough for everyone in the car to hear. Damon in particular. I spent enough time laying blame on myself, I didn't need it from him.

"I didn't ask for what happened to me." No matter how deserved I felt it was, my punishment could have been less extreme. Less traumatising.

"No one said you did," Damon said coolly. "I don't want the boss or Gianni getting killed because they're too busy thinking with their cocks." He glared at a driver who tried to change lanes without indicating.

"Them or you?" I retorted.

Damon didn't respond.

Yeah, that was what I thought.

Gianni chuckled and even Reuben snorted softly. Neither seemed worried about any feelings Damon or his cock had for me.

I sank back into my seat and closed my eyes. During my darkest days back in the cage, right after Kurt left, I pictured what life outside would be like. I knew better than to picture rainbows and unicorns or any of that bullshit. I pictured my family hating me and wanting nothing to do with me. I imagined them turning their backs on me. Maybe not Asher or Rose, but the rest. They'd give me pitying looks and shake their heads.

All of those thoughts were bleak, but realistic to my troubled mind. My mother used to tell me never to dream beyond what we can actually achieve. She expected all of us to achieve a great deal, and never make excuses when we didn't succeed. If we worked hard enough, we didn't need to have frivolous dreams. Everything was within reach, we just had to believe in our abilities. When we fucked up, it was always our fault. Everything was a lesson in doing better the next time.

Never in a million years would I have expected to

end up here. The sky above me was bluer than I remembered. Food tasted better. Being touched wasn't as terrifying as I'd become accustomed to. But everything was so much more fucking complicated than I would have dreamt. It was hard to believe any man would care about me, or want me, much less three of them.

Damon was right, they could get killed if they let me distract them. He'd never forgive me and I'd never forgive myself. Maybe I should walk away while I still could. Before I fucked up their lives as well as my own. For their sakes, because I cared about them. Because I'd caused enough damage in the past that I didn't want to pay for any more.

Could I walk away? It would take some time and planning. But one thing I knew for sure. I wasn't going anywhere until I knew Kurt was dead. I needed these three men and their resources to make sure he, and anyone working for him, was gone for good.

Unless…

I chewed my lip and toyed with my options. The first of those was seeing if the man the twins were watching was Kurt.

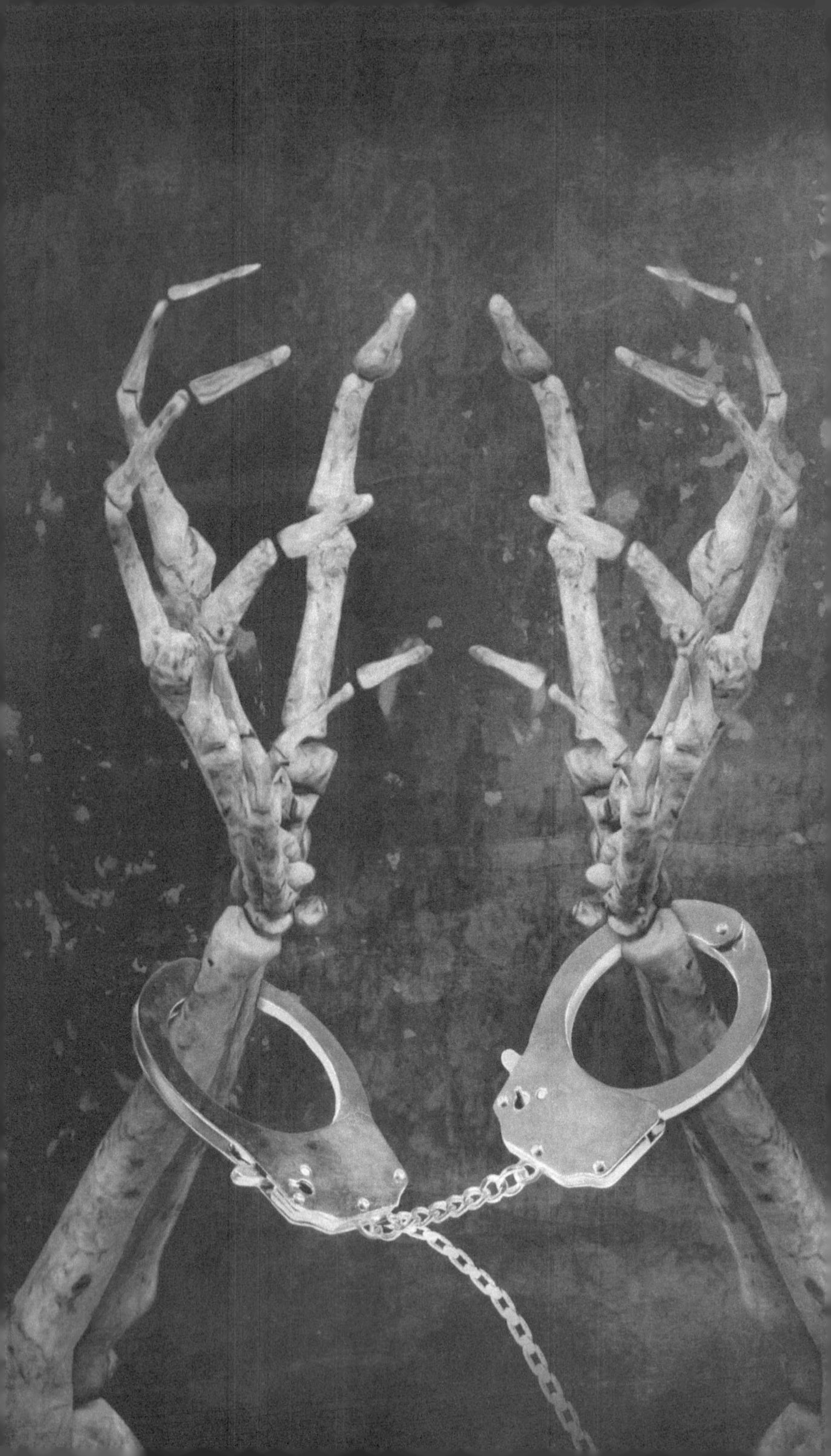

CHAPTER 19

MINA

"Asshole is in there." Hunter leaned closer to a streetlight and jerked his head towards the house at the end of the street.

A light was on, but I couldn't make out anyone inside.

From the outside, the house looked no different to any other in the area. Small, single story, driveway big enough for one car. The bushes at the front were neatly trimmed, as was a short section of grass between the house and the road.

"We didn't get close enough to confirm whether or not it's him," Parker said.

"That's right," Hunter said. "When the notification popped up, we picked him up from near the airport. He matches the description of the asshole on the security camera."

"So he could be anyone?" Damon asked.

"He could be, but my spidey senses tell me otherwise," Hunter said. "And the fact he tried to throw us off his tail three times on the way here. If that doesn't say guilty as shit, nothing else would."

"Sounds guilty as shit to me," Gianni agreed. "I see he didn't manage to lose you."

Parker grinned. "You have to be smarter than this guy to outsmart us."

"Kurt is smart enough to have eluded us up until now," Reuben said. He leaned against the side of his car, his gaze intent on the small house as though he could look right inside.

"Until now, being the key words here," Hunter said. "He wasn't going to be able to do it forever."

"What are you thinking?" Gianni asked me softly.

I blinked a couple of times. "The same thing you're thinking."

He nodded. "This is much too easy."

"Tracking that dickhead here wasn't easy," Parker said. He didn't exactly bristle, but his tone was this side of offended.

"For someone who got away with what he did for so long, it was," Gianni reasoned. "Something about this is off."

"You think this is a trap," Damon stated.

Gianni glanced at him. "You don't? This isn't what you'd do if you were Kurt?"

I shuddered. Damon was prickly, but he was nothing like Kurt.

"If I was that shithead, I'd stay as far away from us as I could get," Damon said. "I'd be well aware my days were numbered. I wouldn't bother trying to lure us into anything."

"Unless he believes he has something up on us," I said. "Some way to convince us to stop hunting him." I wouldn't be surprised what depths he'd sink to in order to get what he wanted.

"Nothing exists that would stop me," Reuben said. "There's nothing he could say, do or threaten."

"What if he was holding Parker and me hostage?" Hunter asked.

Reuben arched an eyebrow at him.

Hunter winced. "Ouch. Thanks a lot, big brother. We love you too."

"Since it's clear he isn't holding you ransom, you're being offended for no reason," Reuben said. He seemed particularly unimpressed.

"It was hypothetical," Hunter grumbled.

Parker put an arm around his twin's shoulders. "You know Reuben would do whatever he had to do to get us free. He just likes to play with us and piss us off. It's his favourite pastime. Maybe it's our fault for telling him to get a hobby. He made this his."

Reuben grunted, but didn't take the bait any further. "Get closer and see if it is Kurt." He nodded to the twins and Gianni, before gesturing for Damon and me to stay with him.

"I can go too," I argued. "If it is him, I need to see." I

wouldn't be surprised if Gianni or the twins killed him on sight. I wanted to see him before they could. I wanted to be the one to kill him.

"Mina," Reuben said, his voice even lower than usual.

"Nothing is going to happen to me," I said. "Not with Gianni, Hunter and Parker there too."

"We'll be fine too," Parker said. "Thanks so much for caring."

Reuben glanced at him and smirked.

Parker just grinned and shrugged in response.

Reuben closed his eyes and exhaled, his breath reluctant at best. "If anything happens to you—"

"The twins better be dead first," Gianni finished for him.

"Hey," Hunter protested. "Not you too, Gianni. I thought we were friends."

Gianni grinned. "I'm just saying, that's all. The only way anyone gets to her is through us. For what it's worth, I'd be dead too."

I caught Damon glowering in my direction. Clearly he hadn't changed his stance that I was a distraction. This whole conversation was a perfect example.

I reached into the back of the car, opened the box and pulled out two knives. Without another word, I headed through the darkness, toward the house.

"Shit." Gianni hurried to catch up. The twins weren't far behind.

"Just remember it might not be him," Gianni said as

we stepped past the other houses and slowed. As tempting as it was to break down the front door, it wasn't subtle and he was right.

I didn't want another innocent person to get hurt or killed because of me.

"At this point, I don't give a shit if it is him or not," Hunter said. "I'm enjoying myself. The expression on Reuben's face was fucking priceless." He offered his twin a fist bump.

"Enjoy it quieter," Gianni said. "Both of you go around the back. See if you can find a window to look through." He took my hand and pulled me down into the shadows near some bushes.

I forced myself not to flinch, or squeeze his hand for reassurance. I needed to be cool, calm and rational right now. Anything else would be dangerous for all of us.

The twins nodded before slipping away into the darkness.

"Call me crazy, but this shit is the most fun part of the job to me," Gianni whispered. "The anticipation of what might come next is next level."

"I like knowing exactly what's coming next," I whispered back.

I preferred careful planning and a flawless execution, to running into a situation and hoping for the best. Sometimes the latter was all you could do, but the former was easier to control.

Admittedly, it was almost impossible to control every aspect of anything. With that in mind, I was always flexible and watching for unexpected variables.

"I like coming," Gianni said lightly. "Especially when you're involved."

I snorted softly. Everything had to come back to sex, didn't it?

"It's not my fault if situations like this turn me on," he added. "With you next to me, it's even hotter." He adjusted the front of his pants and looked pained. Judging by the tenting, he was ready to go again.

"You're not planning to sneak off and fuck are you?" Parker asked. He slipped back through the shadows and crouched beside us. "He's still in there, but I can't make out anything more than a shape moving around. There's blinds on the back of the house that don't have convenient peepholes in them. So inconsiderate."

"I knew this guy was an asshole." Hunter crouched beside Parker. "He could have left one of the blinds open."

"How thoughtless of him to want privacy," I said sarcastically. Kurt didn't deserve any, but if it wasn't him, then we shouldn't be peeking in. There might be an innocent woman or child on the other side of that blind. The twins hadn't mentioned seeing anyone else, but that didn't necessarily mean they weren't here.

"She gets it." Hunter offered me a fist bump.

I brushed my fist over his before quickly pulling it back. "I guess we're going to have to do this a different way."

"The direct route," Gianni agreed. "We walk right up to the front door and knock. I know, it's an old-fashioned thing to do, but I think we can pull it off."

"Knocking on the front door is so lame," Parker complained.

"Yes, it is, but that's what we're going to do," Gianni said. "At least, that's what I'm going to do. The three of you are going to stay here."

Before anyone could argue, he rose and strode toward the door like he had every reason to be there.

Without hesitating, I rose and followed him.

"I told you to stay back there," Gianni said conversationally.

"So you did," I said. "I decided not to. Kurt knows what you look like."

"He knows what you look like too," Gianni said. "If he tries anything, you should be far enough away to be able to run."

"I want to be close enough to stop him," I said. "You know what I can do with a knife."

"I also know you're traumatised by what he did." Gianni stopped short of the front steps. "Trauma and fear can make people hesitate."

He was right, but not in this situation. I couldn't let myself freak out. If I did, Kurt won. Fuck that.

"I won't hesitate," I insisted. "I can do this. Not to mention, there's nothing you could say that would make me back away now. We're doing this."

He sighed out his nose. "Woman, you're making me

hard as fuck again. Fine, just be careful, okay? The longer this goes on, the more desperate Kurt will be. The more desperate he is, the more chance there is that he'll do something stupid. The stupider it is, the more likelihood we die. The more dead we are, the better chance I haunt his ass. No one wants that because I will be noisy as fuck." His teeth flashed white in the darkness.

"I'll be careful," I promised. "I don't want either of us to end up dead." The reality of that surprised me. At some point during the last few weeks, I'd started wanting to live again. I had things to live for now. Hope that my life wasn't a complete cluster fuck. I also really, really didn't want Gianni to die. The idea made my heart hurt.

"Okay, let's do this." He slipped his hand into mine and we took the front steps together, side-by-side.

A single light illuminated the front door. Painted off-white, it looked fresh, as though the whole house was recently renovated.

Gianni tapped on the door.

A shuffling came from inside the house, followed by footsteps.

"If you're looking for Courtney she's not—" The door slid open smoothly.

My heart bottomed out. The man standing just inside the door wasn't Kurt, but the resemblance was strong enough to knock the breath out of my body.

"We're not looking for Courtney," Gianni said easily,

like they were having a pleasant chat. "Although, she's a lovely person. Really sweet. No, we were looking for someone else. A guy named Gustav. I know he lives around here somewhere. Do you know which house is his?" He twisted his upper body and gestured back toward the street.

The man looked confused. "I don't know no Gustav. I only just moved in here, I don't know anyone in the area. How do you know Courtney?" His eyes narrowed like he was trying to figure out what Gianni's angle was. And if he could get the door closed fast enough.

Gianni grinned. "I don't, I was just guessing. You seem like the kind of guy who likes his women sweet. I mean, don't we all?" He glanced over at me.

I smirked in response. I wouldn't consider myself to be sweet. Anything but.

"I guess so," the man said uncertainly. "Like I said, I can't help you."

"That's a shame," Gianni said. "That's okay though, we'll keep looking. He must be around here somewhere. A guy like Gustav is difficult to hide. He's the kind who stands out in a crowd, if you know what I mean." He turned away from the door and back towards the steps.

Before I followed, I pinned the man with a look. "Do you know Kurt Lasalle?"

His brief moment of hesitation was all the answer I needed.

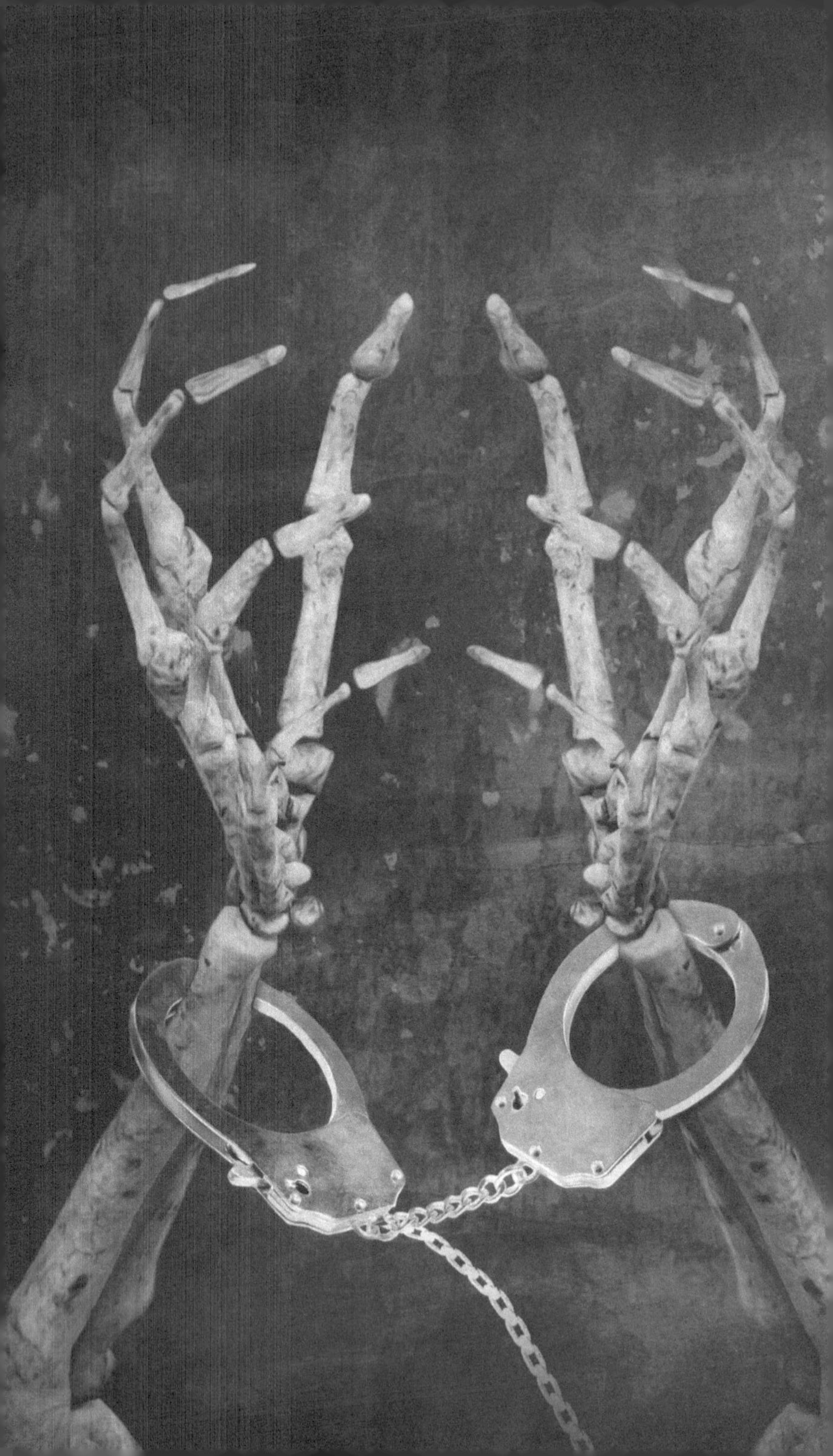

CHAPTER 20

MINA

Before he could take another breath, I had a knife to his throat and was pushing him back into the house, my fingertips barely touching his chest.

He stepped back so fast he almost tripped and fell. He spread his arms to either side to balance himself and lunged for a gun that lay on a table beside the door.

"Don't fucking touch it," I said. The tip of my knife was right against his jugular. It would be a simple matter to slice it open.

He froze, his hand hovered over it before he pulled his arms back in.

"Where is he?" I snarled.

"I don't know," he stammered. "I swear. He contacted me through a mutual acquaintance. Offered me ten grand to come here. That was all. I never met him and I don't know why he wanted me to come here."

His voice was high. He seemed ready to piss his pants.

"Who is this mutual acquaintance?" I asked.

"Let me guess." Gianni followed us inside. "Courtney?"

"I never met her either," he insisted. "She was some chick I met online. For all I know, she doesn't even exist. I needed the money, that's all I fucking know. I'll swear on anything you want. My phone is over there, on the table. You can see all the conversations I had with her." He jerked his head to the side.

"Pick it up," I said. If this was some kind of trap, the phone could be hiding a bomb or who knows what else.

He inched over, scooped up the phone and offered it to me.

"Open it," I said.

He hesitated.

Gianni scooped up the man's gun from the table and aimed it at his temple. "You heard the woman."

The man swallowed, but tapped on the screen to open the phone and enter the message app. He offered it to me, but Gianni took it first.

"Let's see what this motherfucker has to say for himself."

"Are you having fun without us?" Hunter stepped inside the house, Parker behind him.

"It looks like it," Parker said. "I like a woman who knows how to handle a knife."

"Don't even think about it or you won't be able to

handle anything ever again," Gianni said pleasantly. "You'll find life more difficult without hands."

Parker chuckled. "Chill out, I was just making an observation."

Gianni grunted and returned his attention to the phone. "Dick pics? Really? You're old enough to know better."

"I thought she was legit," the man whined.

"Well, StudMuffin69, I think you've been had," Gianni said. "Or should I say, Frank."

"Stud muffin?" Hunter cracked up laughing. "He wishes."

I ignored him. "Is there any indication of where Kurt is right now? Some reason why he set this up?"

"My guess is he hired Frank here as a distraction." Gianni tossed the phone back on the table. "I don't think he knows Jack shit."

"I really don't," Frank said frantically. "All I know is what you saw there. I was told to take that flight to Sydney, make sure those two noticed me and come here." He tilted his head towards the twins, the movement subtle and nervous.

"Was he supposed to contact you with more instructions?" I directed the question at Frank and Gianni.

"If there's anything else, he deleted it," Gianni said. "Or Kurt hasn't contacted him again yet."

"Parker and I will report to Reuben," Hunter said. "He'll want to know if this has something to do with us and not Mina."

I watched Frank's eyes for any reaction to Hunter saying my name, but discerned nothing. If this was anything to do with me, he didn't know about it.

"Now, what do we do with Frank here?" Gianni asked. He picked the phone back up and tucked it into his pocket. "If Kurt tries to contact him, he can go through me. But it seems to me that if Frank doesn't know anything, he's no use to us."

"Please," Frank groaned. He swallowed hard. "I don't know anything, I swear. You have my phone, I can't contact him again. I don't know where he is. Fuck, I don't even know *who* he is. He might not be real either."

I wished he wasn't, but he was, and the reality was that he'd want to speak to Frank about this whole incident. After Kurt ran, he might have assumed I died in that cage. Frank seeing me would be proof that didn't happen.

But only if I left him alive.

I pressed the blade more firmly against his throat.

"Daddy?" A small voice came from the back of the room.

I looked away from Frank, to see a girl of five or six years old, standing in what looked like a bedroom doorway. She wore pyjamas that covered her feet, so she was head to toe in pink and purple unicorns. Her dark hair was messy, her eyes looked heavy with sleep. We must have woken her up.

"What the hell?" Gianni whispered, echoing my thoughts.

"It's okay, Holly, go back to bed. Everything will be okay." Frank slid a smile in her direction, trying to be reassuring while clearly scared out of his wits.

It was my turn to freeze. My mind went back to a night a bit over five years ago.

A tangle of dark curls. Huge eyes that looked back at me with no hint of understanding.

She shouldn't have been there.

She wasn't part of the plan.

I should have known.

I should have anticipated.

I should have been able to stop myself.

The blood on my hands was hers. I never meant to spill a drop, but I had. She died in my arms. I felt the life slip away from her. Bit by bit, drop by drop. There was nothing I could do or say to stop it from happening. The second our lives intersected, hers was over.

Her body went still and cold while I held her. So tiny. Small and innocent and gone. Her pale yellow pyjamas turned sickly orange with her blood. The smiley faces on the fabric grinned at me in accusation. Mocking me.

I fucked up.

I fucked up badly and she paid the price.

I stepped back from Frank and lowered the knife. "No one said anything about a kid."

"Her mother had to work late," Frank said. "She

brought her in through the back so she wouldn't be seen. This wasn't about her."

"No it wasn't," I agreed. "She shouldn't be here." Like that other little girl wasn't supposed to be there that night. She was dead because of it. Like Holly would have been if Kurt set a trap for us all.

"I'll take her home," Frank said. "I don't need to be here either." He stepped backward towards the little girl. Held out his hand to her.

"Word of advice," Gianni said. "Stay away from creeps on the Internet. There's a lot of shady people out there. You got paid?"

"Yeah," I did," Frank said. Holly slipped her hand into his.

"Then take it and get out of here," Gianni said. "Don't talk about what happened here and don't look back."

Frank picked up Holly and rested her on his hip. "No one will hear about this from me. I swear that on my daughter's life." She clearly meant everything to him. He wouldn't say anything to anyone, if only because we knew she existed too. Some people wouldn't hesitate to use a child to further themselves. Especially someone like Kurt. I didn't want to think about what he might do to her if he got anywhere near her.

I put the knife away and watched while they hurried to gather Holly's things and slip out the back door.

"You okay, sweetheart?" Gianni asked. "You look like you saw a ghost when that kid appeared."

"I didn't expect to see her there," I said. That much was true. The rest was something I wasn't ready to talk about yet. What would he think of me if he knew? My own father sent me to Kurt when he found out. If someone who was supposed to love me would do that, then there was nothing I could put past anyone, no matter their feelings for me. I may find myself back in that cage, or dead.

No, that was better kept to myself.

"I'll be having words with those twins about missing that piece of vital information," Gianni said. He twirled the gun around his middle finger.

I might have a few with them myself. In the meantime, I had more questions than answers. Why had Kurt wanted Frank to lead the twins here? I remembered what Daze said about him being smart and meticulous. There was no way in hell he'd do all of this for no reason. If he wanted to distract us, then there was something he wanted us to be distracted from. What the fuck was he up to?

"Come on, Reuben and Damon will want to know you're okay." Gianni took a step towards the door.

Before he stepped outside, he stopped and turned around. "I might not be the handsomest or smartest guy around, but I know when something is up. I saw the expression on your face when you saw that kid. Something happened. I don't give a shit what it was but I'll tell you this."

He pointed a finger in the direction of my nose. "It wasn't your fault. All of this, it might just have been some kind of set up. Some way for that prick to fuck with your head. If that's all it was, don't let him get to you. He doesn't deserve to live rent-free in your head. He deserves a fucking bullet in his."

He lowered his hand and nodded once like that was that, end of story.

I pressed my lips together and rolled them a couple of times. "You might be biased."

He didn't know the circumstances and he wasn't going to hear them from me tonight.

He was guessing, based on his feelings for me. Feelings that were sweet, but were they misplaced?

Seeing that kid standing there tonight brought everything back into painfully sharp focus. Maybe Kurt was fucking with me, but he'd succeeded in rattling me. He'd gotten right back into my head. Reminding me of who and what I was.

I wasn't sweet little Mina anymore. I hadn't been for a long time. Longer than most people knew. Everyone except my father, and a couple of other people, including Kurt.

"If I'm biased, I don't give a shit," Gianni said. "I meant what I said. Whatever the fuck went down, I don't blame you for it. Not even if anyone else does, you've more than paid the price. I'll fucking tell them all that too."

He fixed me with a look like that was that, whether I liked it or not. His determination was endearing, as was his blind faith. He'd made up his mind and no one and nothing was going to change it for him. Or so he thought. The reality might end up being very different. He might end up being the one with his heart torn clean out of his chest.

"Yeah," I said softly.

We stepped out the front door of the house and back down the steps.

We reached the street as Frank bundled Holly into a small hatchback. The vehicle looked old enough to back up his story about needing money. It had definitely seen better days.

He glanced over his shoulder at us before quickly jumping into the driver's seat. The door slammed behind him with a thud before he roared off down the street and was gone.

A heartbeat later, the house beside us exploded into flames.

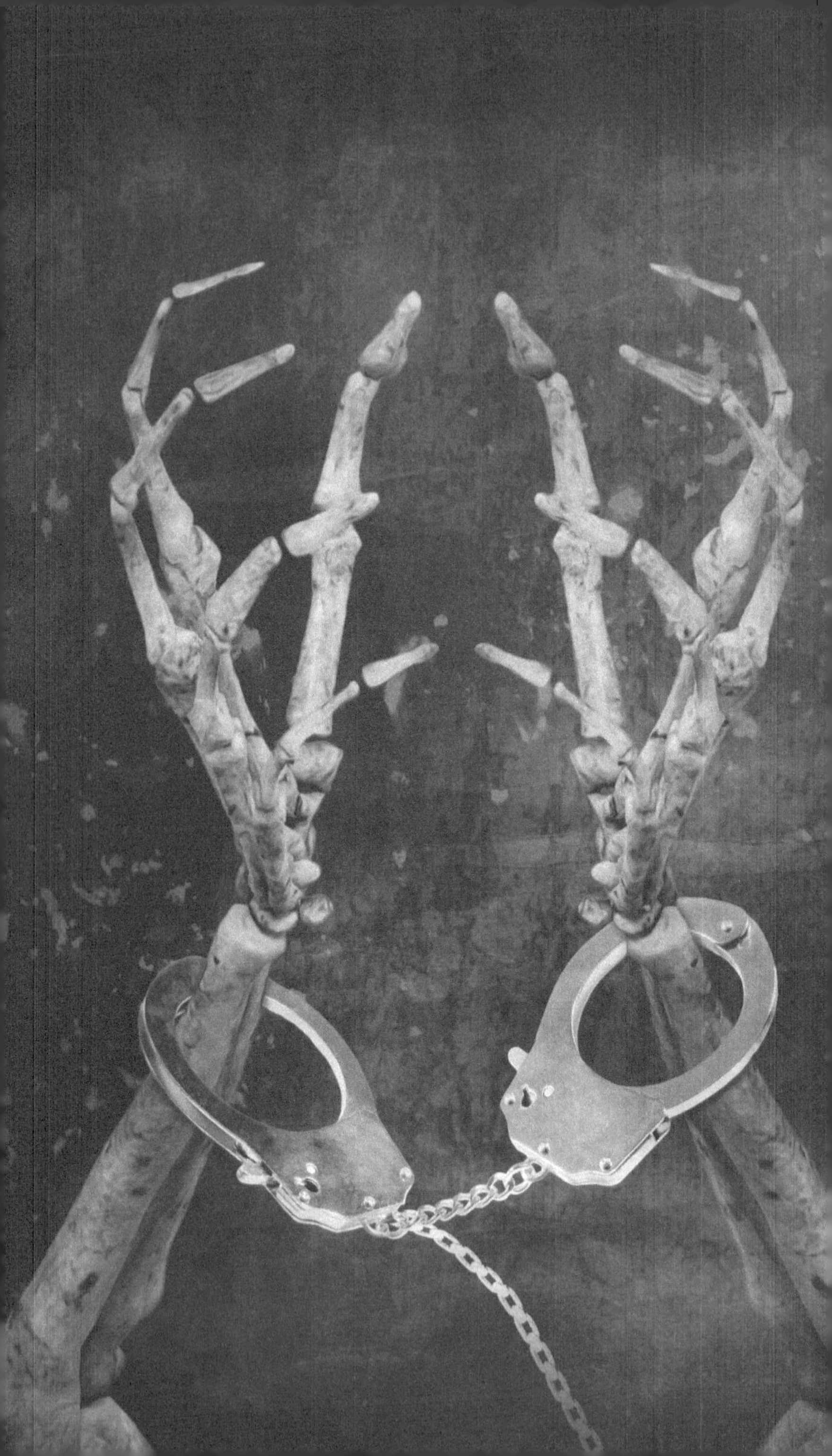

CHAPTER 21

MINA

Gianni pushed me off my feet and threw himself over me, arms wrapped around me tight.

I landed on the footpath with a thud, forced my eyes shut, and curled up as small as I could.

He let out a grunt of pain. His ragged breath was hot on the side of my face. Fingers dug into my hip, holding frantically while hell rained down behind us.

I heard a shout, but couldn't make out the words past the ringing in my ears.

Gianni's body pressed against me was overwhelming. Conflicting. Both comforting and terrifying at the same time.

Finally, everything fell. Everything but the pounding in my heart and the roaring of blood through my veins.

"Mina?" Reuben's voice sounded distant, like he was talking through a tunnel.

Someone helped Gianni to his feet. His weight was suddenly gone from me.

I opened my eyes and squinted.

Reuben crouched beside me.

"I'm okay." I rolled over and sat up. "Gianni?"

Gianni waved me down. "I'm all good. The back of my shirt might be a little singed." He grabbed the hem and pulled it around to frown at it.

"I'll buy you another shirt," Damon told him. He stood between Gianni and the burning house, flames dancing in the night behind him.

"I knew you cared." Gianni gave him a quick hug before he too crouched down beside me. "You okay, sweetheart?"

"I'm fine," I said vaguely.

My eyes were on the destroyed house. "He did this." I was both horrified and more furious than I ever remembered being. "He knew I'd be here."

"He was probably hoping we'd still be inside," Gianni said.

"The prick seemed to be targeting us." Hunter approached from the shadows, appearing unhurt.

"It does seem a bit personal." Parker was right behind him. "I'm officially offended."

"Me too," Gianni agreed.

"Get out of here," Reuben told the twins. "Gianni, Mina, back in the SUV. I want to be gone from here before the police arrive. Damon, have people move into the area and keep an eye out for Kurt."

"Good idea, boss," Gianni said. He stood with a wince of pain.

Reuben offered me his hand to help me to my feet. His usual closed expression was laced with concern and anger.

"He's fucking with us," I said.

"Or he misjudged," Reuben said quietly. "He might have expected you to be inside for longer."

"Possibly both," Damon suggested. He had his phone to his ear, his expression tight.

Once again, I had more questions than answers. Was he somewhere nearby, deliberately waiting until we were clear before setting up the explosion? Or had he timed it wrong? Did he have any idea a child would be in the house tonight? If he did, he must have known how I'd respond. Was it aimed at me or, like the twins suggested, they were the target?

My lips pressed together, I followed Reuben to the SUV and let him help me inside.

Gianni grimaced, but settled down beside me. "I should say thank you again," I said. "For protecting me. You could have been killed."

"Better me than you, sweetheart," he said. He seemed a lot less cheerful than he usually was. If anything, he seemed rattled. I wouldn't have thought it was possible if I hadn't seen it for myself. Nothing seemed to get to him like this had.

"I'm not that easy to kill." The smile he gave me was forced.

"If we were still inside, or a metre or two closer, we would have been," I said. "Five minutes earlier and he would have killed a child." I watched Gianni's expression carefully.

"Lucky for her he didn't," Gianni said.

"What would you have done if he had?" I asked.

Gianni shrugged. "If she was dead, chances are I would be too."

"But if you weren't?" I pressed. "If you were alive and she was dead, what would you do?"

"In this particular case, we're already hunting him down and want him dead. That hasn't changed." He looked curious as to why I was asking. Enough so that I decided to back off before he was the one with the questions.

"I guess we can't kill him twice," I conceded.

"Technically, we can," he said with a grin. "I have a friend who brought a guy back to life three or four times, just to see how many times he could. But he's a sadistic fuck if I ever met one. On the other hand, that comes with the territory."

"Some people get more enjoyment out of it than others," Damon said from the driver's seat.

"I'd suggest Damon was talking about himself, but I've never known him to get off on other people's suffering," Gianni said.

"Did you just say something nice about me?" Damon asked.

"I guess I did, in a roundabout way," Gianni agreed. "Did you like it?"

"I could get used to you not being an asshole," Damon said.

I leaned my head back against the seat and watched the city lights flash by as we passed.

This whole night was a lot to process. Was Kurt nearby, watching us? I sensed that he wasn't, but no more than that. Without doubt, he'd engineered all of this, but whether things went to plan or not, I had no idea.

I couldn't discount the idea he hoped Reuben and Damon would step into the house with Gianni and me. If that was the case, why not set off the explosion before we left? He would have caught at least two of us if he had.

Although, he'd had five years to kill me if he wanted to. He hadn't. He preferred to toy with me. If that was his plan, then he'd try something else to get to me. If we didn't get to him first.

"We're being followed," Damon said, breaking through my thoughts.

Gianni and I both swivelled around in our seats and looked out the back window. The traffic was light, and the dark vehicle made no attempt to hide the fact they were tailing us.

When Damon turned down a side street, they turned too. When he steered the SUV back onto the main road, they stayed right with us.

They made no attempt to get closer to us until a couple of streets from home. There, they manoeuvred themselves so close the front of their car almost touched the rear of the SUV.

"Hang on," Damon said. He slowed the SUV right down, before pressing his foot hard on the accelerator and jumping forward. He took a bend so fast I thought the tyres on the right-hand side of the car might lift off the road.

I grabbed hold of the handle above the door beside me and held on tight.

Gianni had his gun out, but made no attempt to use it. "Bullet-proof glass," he explained. "Works both ways."

Damon slowed the car down again, and Gianni lowered the window beside him. He stuck his hand out and got off a couple of shots in the direction of the sedan. One hit the side of the windscreen and left a crack, but the sedan didn't slow.

Gianni pulled his hand back in and closed the window. "Fuckers have bullet-proof glass too. I guess they mean business."

"We're not usually followed by people who don't mean business," Reuben said. He sounded as though this happened regularly.

I glanced forward to see him quickly shooting off a text message. A few moments later, his phone flashed with a return message.

"Keep driving," he said. "The twins can be here in three minutes. They're still in the area."

"Got it, boss," Damon said. He resumed driving at a normal speed, weaving through traffic.

I didn't know Sydney well enough anymore to know where we were going, but the traffic and houses gradually thinned, leaving us in a more industrial part of the city. Somewhere less likely to contain crowds or innocent people. Somewhere with less chance of collateral damage. Or, maybe, more places for us to hide.

Reuben's phone lit up again. "The twins are on their tail." For a moment I thought he might leave this to them, but then he said, "Find somewhere to pull over."

"Got it, boss," Damon said again. He didn't question the orders, just drove past a handful of cars and into an empty parking lot in front of a tyre shop.

The car that was tailing us followed us in, another dark sedan right behind them. They must have realised the twins were there, because they turned a tight circle and drove right out of the car park, past the twin's car.

"That was anticlimactic," Gianni remarked.

"You spoke too soon," Damon said.

The sedan stopped sideways across the exit leading out of the car park. The doors opened and several figures stepped out.

"Looks like party time after all," Gianni said. He turned to me. "Is there any chance we can convince you to stay in the car?"

I smiled slightly and pulled out my knives. "Nope."

He sighed dramatically. "That was what I thought. Boss?"

"Keep her safe," was all Reuben said before he opened his own door and stepped out of the SUV.

I slipped out but stayed near the car, using the vehicle as a shield. Just because I'd spent five years living out of the world, didn't mean I was oblivious to the futility of having knives at a gunfight. If I had an opportunity to use them, I would. Otherwise, I'd stay out of the way.

Reuben stayed beside me, Damon and Gianni on either side of us, guns trained on the approaching figures.

In the corner of my eye, I saw the twins get out of their vehicle, guns in their hands.

"This is an interesting place for a chat," Gianni said, loud enough for everyone to hear.

"This isn't a chat." The first of the strangers, a man in his forties with a long chin, said.

"I thought not." Gianni raised his gun and shot him in the centre of his forehead.

The other three dropped back, crouching on the other side of the SUV.

"We came to deliver a message," one of them called out.

"Why can't these motherfuckers learn to text?" came from the direction of the twins. "Even Reuben can text."

"What message?" Damon asked.

"Kurt Lasalle said to back the fuck off."

"We have no intention of backing off," Reuben said coldly. A heartbeat later he said, "Kill them."

Apparently he wasn't in the mood to follow the suggestion of whoever said not to kill the messenger.

Before anyone could move to follow his orders, another two dark sedans stopped behind the first, further blocking the exit.

"Shit just got real," Gianni said.

Damon hummed his agreement. "Too fucking real."

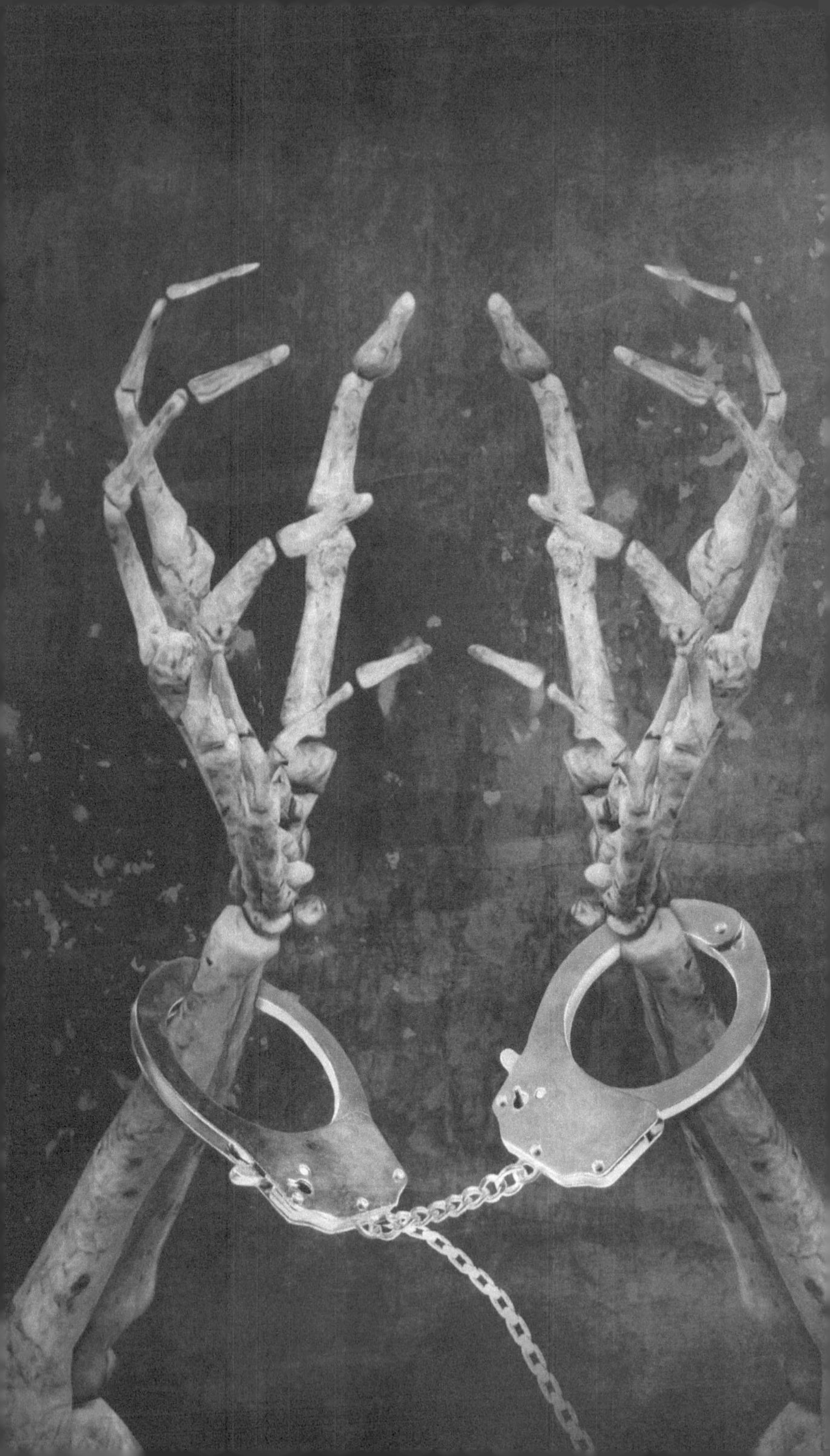

CHAPTER 22

REUBEN

I rubbed a hand over my forehead. A headache threatened. They usually did on nights like this.

I reached into the SUV to pull out a gun for myself. Reluctantly, I handed one to Mina.

I should insist she stay in the car, but under the circumstances, we needed her, and knives would not be enough. Not unless they got a lot closer. None of us had any intention of them getting anywhere near her.

She eyed the gun, but slipped the knives away and took it. As I would have expected of her, she checked to make sure it was loaded and the safety was off. Old, well-learned skills were hard to forget. Impossible with our lifestyle.

I turned my attention back to the new vehicles. Two people stepped out of each one, all on the opposite side, keeping their vehicle between us and them.

Unless others hid in the back, then it was six against seven. Three crouching on the other side of the SUV and four out on the street. We'd faced worse.

Gianni dropped down low and crab-walked silently to the end of the SUV. After a moment, Damon followed. They slid around the front, their movement followed by a painfully loud gunshot, then another.

They threw themselves back behind the SUV.

"One down," Gianni grinned. "One of them almost took a couple of hairs off my head."

Lucky the shot wasn't lower than that.

Without a word, Mina dropped to her stomach on the concrete. For half a second, I thought she'd been shot. That was until the gun in her hand flashed once, twice.

Shouts of pain came from the other side of the vehicle.

"My fucking foot!"

Laughing, Gianni darted back around the front of the SUV and finished off the last two attackers with a shot each.

Damon grunted his approval of Mina's tactic. Injuring them by shooting them in the feet or ankles was the perfect distraction. Unorthodox, but perfect.

She stayed down on the ground, her gun trained on the last two sedans. They were too far away to get a good shot under them, but if the attackers stepped out from behind them, they'd be fair game.

"I told you she was fucking hot." Gianni joined us behind our vehicle. "Foot shot. I'm going to remember that one."

She glanced up at him, but her expression was unreadable. Half a shrug and her attention was back on the car park in front of her.

"We need to draw them out," Damon said. "Can you make it over to the twins' car?"

I nodded. They were a handful of metres away at most, probably growing irritated that they hadn't killed anyone yet. Or at least maimed them. They weren't the kind who got off on killing either, not exactly, but if anyone attacked any of us, they'd want to make them pay. They were a pair of clowns at times, but they had zero tolerance for enemies.

All of us Brantley men had that in common. Even Zeke, although he wouldn't admit it.

"Mina," I said.

She glanced up like she might argue.

"Go with them," Damon told her. When he took that tone, not even I would bother to argue with him. He wouldn't budge.

With a sigh, she rose. She and Gianni bolted a few metres to the other car.

I followed along more slowly. Confident if anyone stepped out to shoot me, they'd end up dead first.

"Nice of you to join us," Hunter said with his usual smug grin. "We were getting lonely over here."

"Hunter was getting lonely," Parker said. "I was getting bored."

"Sorry to disappoint you with the lack of excitement tonight," I said sarcastically. "Next time, I'll organise three explosions and twice the amount of enemies."

Both twins laughed and Gianni chuckled. Mina's expression remained unchanged. She was completely focused on those other two sedans. Laser focused like nothing else in the world was happening right now. I'd only seen her look like that on— I shook my head. That was something I'd have to think about later.

I turned back to my SUV as the engine turned over. Damon put the car into reverse and backed up to the edge of the car park. He revved a couple of times before the car surged forward, flying across the concrete towards the two sedans.

"Holy shit," Gianni said in disbelief.

I silently agreed with them. When Damon suggested a distraction, this wasn't what I thought he had in mind.

The engine roared, the SUV not slowing a hair as it drew closer to the sedans.

At the last second, all four attackers leapt out from behind them, scattering in different directions.

The SUV slammed into the sedans, driving into the gap between them. The front of one and the rear of the other crumpled. They were forced apart with a squeal of steel and the smell of burning rubber.

I was still trying to process what Damon just did

when Gianni and Hunter darted out from behind the vehicle and shot two of the attackers before they could flee.

"Reuben," Mina said in warning.

I turned.

One of the attackers had run around and came up behind us. They barely raised their gun before a knife appeared in the centre of their forehead. Blood blossomed on their skin and their eyes widened before they slumped to the ground.

Mina stood with the other knife in one hand, gun in the other, her hair caked to her temples with sweat. She looked fucking beautiful.

"I don't know where the last one is," she said, eyes scanning the area.

"A long way from here if they have any brains," I said.

She shook her head, the movement so brief I almost missed it. "They're still here."

I knew better than to question instincts when it came to things like this. Instincts kept us alive. Her instincts saved my life. If she said they were here, then they were.

I stayed perfectly still, also scanning the area. Whatever she sensed, I felt nothing, but I was better at giving orders than I was at this. I had no trouble admitting that. My skills were different, not flawed.

"Stay there," she whispered.

"I don't—" I started to say.

She cut me off with a look. "I can do this. Stay here."

If anyone else spoke to me that way, I'd growl at them. Her tone and the look on her face convinced me to nod and stay back near the car.

"Be safe," was all I could say.

She nodded in return and slipped away into the darkness.

"Where did she go?" Gianni asked. He had one eye on me and the other on the SUV. Clearly torn between protecting me and staying near Mina, and seeing if Damon was okay.

"I don't—" I was interrupted by a grunt from several metres away. That was followed by a thud. "There, I think. Go check on Damon." It was clearly not a female grunt. Not Mina's anyway. That should account for all of them.

Gianni hesitated, then nodded. "On it, boss." Gun still in his hand, he trotted to the SUV, followed by the twins.

I waited until Mina returned a minute or two later. She looked exhausted.

"That's the last of them," she confirmed. "He was trying to sneak up on you. Or on me." She shrugged. "Either way, he won't be sneaking anywhere again."

She made to trudge past me towards where the others were helping Damon out of the SUV. As far as I could tell, he was unhurt, apart from a few bruises.

In spite of the impact, the front of the SUV protected him. Of course it did, I paid good money to have vehicles that would stand up to anything we put them through. Bullets, crashes, explosions. That was money well spent.

I reached out and grabbed Mina's elbow. Even when she flinched, I didn't let it go.

"Take a moment," I said softly. "Damon is okay."

"I'm not—" she started to say.

"You're as tired as the rest of us," I said. "More so. You're still recovering."

She stopped and turned back to me. Her focused, professional mask eased somewhat, if it didn't melt away completely.

"Everyone is okay." She blinked as though suddenly realising that.

"Everyone is fine, thanks to you," I said. "And Damon." And Gianni too, but she and Damon were exceptional tonight.

She seemed to crumble a little. Her throat bobbed as she swallowed hard.

Taking the chance that I wouldn't freak her out, I wrapped my arms around her and pulled her to my chest.

She hesitated for a moment before leaning into me and letting herself be held.

I rubbed a hand up and down her back and held her as tight as I dared. If she was anyone else, I would have expected her to cry, but she didn't. She just let me hold her while she composed herself again.

She fit perfectly into the circle of my arms, like she

was made to be there. The scent of her was more addictive than anything I'd ever experienced before. I wanted to inhale enough of it to imprint it on my mind forever.

She finally pulled back and looked up at me. "Just another regular Tuesday?"

I snorted softly. "Fuck no. This is more like a regular Thursday. Tuesdays are usually quieter."

She grimaced but managed a short laugh. "Remind me to stay in the library and read on a Thursday night."

"And miss a chance to see Damon crash a car like a fucking rally driver?" Gianni had his arm over Damon's shoulders as they approached us. "That was fucking epic. I don't know who made me harder tonight, Mina or Damon. It might be a tie."

"We all know it was me," Hunter said from behind them. "I have that effect on everyone."

"You don't have that effect on me," Parker told him.

Hunter made a face. "Thank fuck for that."

I rolled my eyes at them. "Both of you can get out of here now."

They gave me identical, meaningful looks.

I sighed. "Thank you for coming to help. Even though it's what I pay you for. And neither of you did what Damon did. Or what Mina did. Or—"

"You're welcome," they both said before I could finish. They high-fived each other before getting back into their car and driving the car up a section of gutter, over grass and back onto the street.

I shook my head. If anything in my life was

constant, it was those two and how ridiculous they could be. But they were here when we needed them and that was what mattered.

I made a mental note to give them both a pay raise. In a week or two, when all of this was forgotten.

"I'll drive," Gianni said. "Damon can sit in the back and relax."

"I should be grumpy about the scratches on my SUV," I said. "But, good work. That took some balls." I didn't really give a fuck about scratches or dents on a piece of equipment. They were easily replaced. The people I could trust were not. They were few and far between as it was.

Damon nodded. "I had to prove mine were bigger than Gianni's somehow." His expression was perfectly deadpan.

"If you wanted to compare ball size, you only had to ask," Gianni said. "I'd happily show you mine." He patted the front of his jeans.

"Maybe later." Damon trudged back to the SUV and all but fell into the back.

"That wasn't a no," Gianni pointed out. "Maybe I could rub your back for you when we get home. We'd hate for those muscles to tighten up after crashing a perfectly good car."

He grinned and opened the other back door for Mina.

She let me walk over with her and help her into the back. I didn't want to let her go, but I had to step back and let Gianni close the door. The feeling of holding her like that was going to linger on my senses for a long time.

I was going to need a long shower and my hand on my cock to get any sleep tonight.

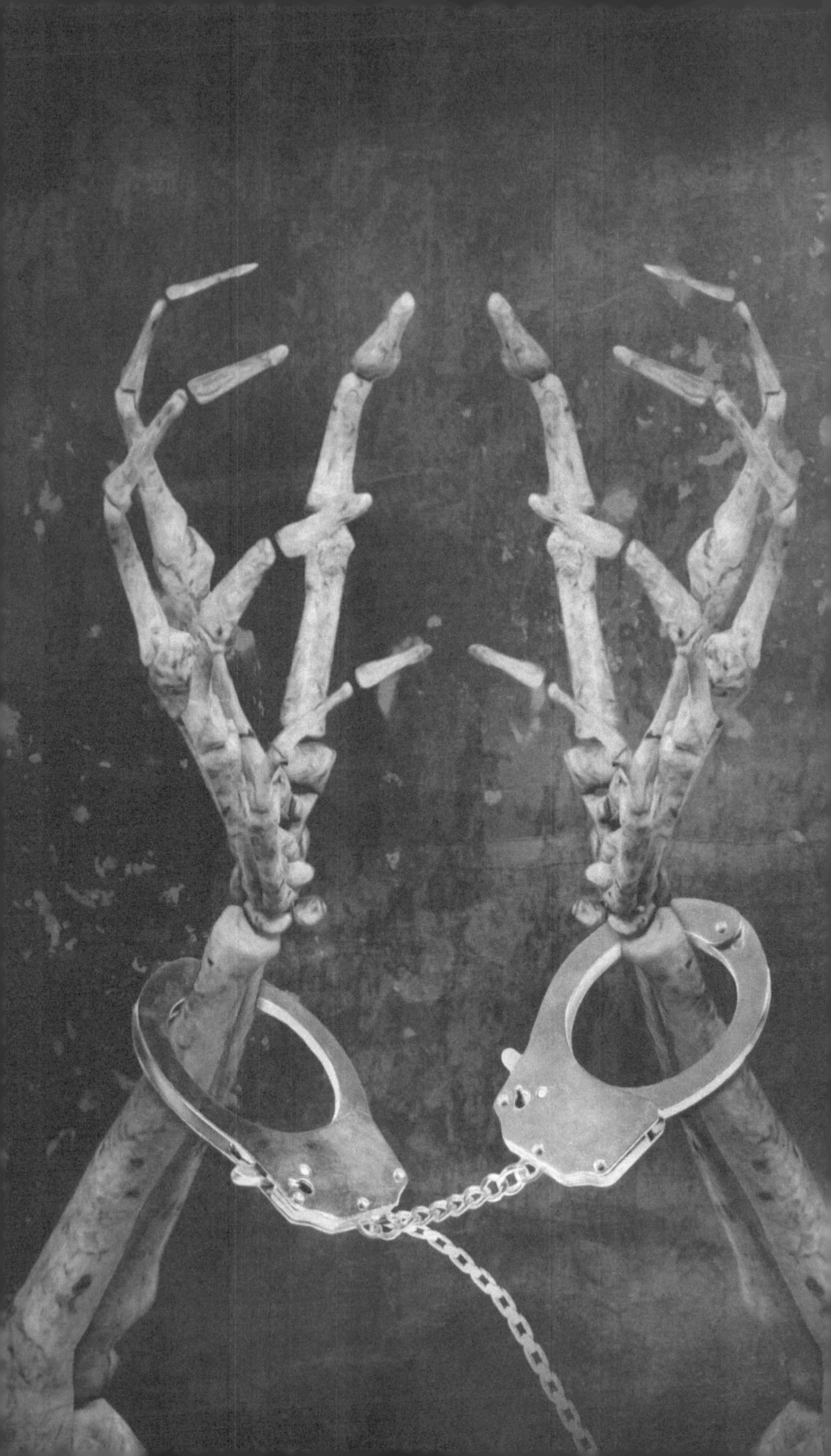

CHAPTER 23

MINA

I held my mug in both hands, half-watching the steam rise off my tea.

"That was a hell of a thing you did." I glanced over to Damon, who sat hunched over the table.

He shrugged one shoulder. "I knew the SUV was up to it." He sipped a drink which was more alcohol than coffee.

"You could have been wrong," I pointed out.

He looked back over to me and scoffed before turning back to his drink. "I wasn't."

"If you were, you'd be dead now. Or worse." I blew lightly on the steam and watched it dance away.

I hadn't been able to sleep, so I figured I'd come down here and have something that might relax me. It seemed he had the same problem.

"I'm sure you wouldn't have minded too much," he said. "If I was dead, I mean."

"It helped us to get out alive," I said lightly. Of course I didn't want him dead, or injured, but if he was going to play the grumpy asshole, I'd play along.

He turned back to me and smirked. "That's what's important. Princess Mina walking away unhurt."

I rolled my eyes. "Please, I'm no more a princess than you are. We both know why you did what you did."

He swivelled around and propped his elbow on the table. "Why don't you enlighten me? Don't try to paint me as some fucking hero."

"Why not?" I asked. "Is there something wrong with doing a brave thing? Whether or not you thought the SUV was up to smashing headfirst into another two cars, it's above your pay grade." I stopped and crinkled my brow. "You're right. Now I think about it, it was a dumbass move. You could have gotten yourself killed and wrecked a perfectly good car."

He arched an eyebrow at me.

"But you did it because you care," I said slowly. "Because, at the end of the day, this is a family. Reuben is more than a boss to you. Gianni is more than a co-worker. The twins too, I'm guessing." I sipped my tea and watched his expression.

"Could be," he said. "Or I'm a reckless dumbass who gets off on driving fast and smashing shit up."

"Maybe both," I said. "I didn't say you weren't a dumbass that cared."

He grunted. "You're making me out to be something

I'm not. Someone had to do something and I did. That's all there was to it. Nothing fucking more and nothing fucking less."

"If you say so," I said lightly.

"I do say so." He turned away again.

"Why is it so difficult to accept that someone appreciates something you did?" I asked.

"Reuben told me you went off by yourself to kill the last of the attackers," Damon said, his voice low. "What did you do? Cut their throat like you did with that woman?"

My pulse sped up, blood thudding through my ears like it had when I walked through the darkness, hunting before I struck.

"Yes, I did. It was the quickest and cleanest thing I could do at the time. The most efficient."

"Why did you do it?" He turned back around to face me. "You could have let them come to you. Reuben or Gianni would have shot them. You didn't have to do a thing."

He was trying to bait me. To make me admit that I did what had to be done. As if somehow that would lessen what he did. I wasn't going to take it.

"I did it because I didn't want anyone else getting hurt," I said. "Because this is my family too."

"Even though you could have been killed," he said. "You don't think that was reckless?"

I didn't think that in the slightest. I knew what I was

capable of. Dealing with one attacker who didn't see me coming was almost effortless.

"I wasn't thinking about myself," I said. "The same way you weren't thinking about yourself. We did what we had to do to protect the people we care about. They did the same for us."

He made an indeterminate sound in the back of his throat and picked up his drink to take a gulp. It looked like half of it went down in one swallow.

"You don't think they care about you?" I asked. "Because I can tell you, they do. Gianni will tell you that himself. Reuben is more...reserved. He doesn't trust easily, but he trusts you. Even when you're being a grumpy asshole. Which, as far as I can tell, is most of the time."

He responded with a side eye. "You think I should be more warm and fuzzy like Gianni or the twins? That's not who I am. No more than it is who you are. Not anymore."

He took in my look of surprise. "I met you before. At least, I was present. Reuben went to talk to your father and you came into the room. It was like the fucking sun rose in the middle of the night. But not anymore."

He might as well have taken a needle and stabbed me right in the heart with it. His aim was perfect, the target hit dead on.

"We all change," I murmured. "I had to grow up sometime. Even if Kurt wasn't—"

"But he was," Damon interrupted. "Do you know

why everyone bought the story about you running off to marry some nice guy and living in the suburbs? It wasn't because your father was convincing. It was because we thought it was the truth. Because a girl like you doesn't belong in *this* world. You should be baking birthday cakes for sweet little babies who grow up never knowing how to use a gun. You should be going to school plays and ballet recitals. Soccer games on Sunday morning and watching Disney movies a hundred times over.

"You shouldn't be sneaking around in the dark and cutting throats, or trying to find some asshole who locked you up in hell and tortured you until you became the shadow instead of the sunshine. I've seen some fucked up stuff in my day, but what he did to you is by far the worst. And to the person who deserves it the least."

For the first time in years, I found tears trickling down my cheeks. He was so wrong and so right at the same time. Everyone had the impression I was sweet and innocent, but it was a façade. It was a role I played so well no one thought to look for me. No one thought anything bad could happen to that sweet girl.

"I'm not the sweet person you think I am," I managed to say.

His lips moved as he thought about how to respond to that. Finally he said, "Probably not. You know how to throw a knife and use a gun. You don't flinch when Reuben orders us to kill. It's possible that if it wasn't for Kurt, you would have become as jaded as me in time."

I stepped over to lower myself into the chair beside him. "It's also possible the girl you think you saw never existed. You've had years to build her up in your mind and make her something else."

"I know what I saw," he said with a grunt. "What I don't understand is why your father handed you over to that fucking prick. It was clear for everyone to see that he adored you. You were his favourite. His princess."

A knot in the table became absolutely fascinating for a minute or two. I focused on it and let his words rattle around in my brain.

"He had a debt," I said eventually. "He had to pay it."

"He had money," Damon insisted. "What could be so big or important that he had to give up his favourite daughter?"

"You might be wrong that I was his favourite," I suggested. "Have you met Rose? He adored her. And Dane and Asher. Just like tonight, he did what he had to do."

Damon shook his head. "I don't buy it."

"It doesn't matter whether you do or not," I said, sharper than I intended. I didn't want to break this fragile truce between us, but he couldn't keep pushing the way he was. I couldn't give him the answers he needed. Not tonight. No matter how much I wanted to tell him everything. I couldn't guarantee he wouldn't turn on me the moment I stepped foot out of the kitchen. Or before.

He sat back. "I guess it doesn't. " His stony expression was back in place. "All those years is enough time to trick myself into thinking someone is different to how they really are." He clearly didn't believe that either. If he did, that would mean questioning his own memory and judgement. In his line of work, that was a dangerous slope to get onto. One that was difficult to get off again alive.

"It's nice to know you were thinking of me," I said lightly. "I must have made quite the impression."

That wasn't the point he was making here, but I couldn't resist the gentle dig. It seemed as though he'd given me a lot of consideration over the years. Now I thought back, I remembered seeing him with Reuben. He was sullen and stayed in the background, much like he was now. Much like many of my father's visitors were.

He smirked. "Short skirt, cute tits, fuckable mouth, it's hard to forget. Don't flatter yourself too much, I just pictured you riding my dick, that's all."

I returned his smirk. "If you say so." That was not all and we both knew it.

Although, that may have been part of it. I *was* cute and confident back then. Happy and comfortable in my skin. As comfortable as anyone could be at eighteen.

Now— Calling me a shadow wasn't inaccurate. I was a shadow of my old self. If you showed me photos of me back then, I'd probably struggle to recognise myself. Especially if I compared them to my reflection in the mirror.

"You're still a distraction," he said.

"You're still an asshole," I retorted. If he wasn't going to give me a centimetre of leeway, then I wasn't giving him any either. Although, there wasn't as much animosity behind either of our words as there was before.

The sides of his mouth tugged up just a fraction. "Yes, I am. Don't forget it. I'm a reckless asshole who likes to drive too fast and smash perfectly good cars. I missed my calling. I could have done that professionally."

"I'm guessing this pays better," I said. "And you get to be surrounded by family."

"There are worse ways to live," he conceded. "Or die."

I raised my mug and toasted him. He raised his and tapped it against mine.

"I propose we don't die anytime soon," I said. "In fact, I refuse to die until I know Kurt is dead." However long that took, I didn't care. Until I saw him dead with my own eyes, I wouldn't fully relax, and I sure as hell didn't plan to die. After everything, I wouldn't give him the satisfaction.

Damon hummed. "That sounds like a good ambition to me. I think I'll do that too. Although, I might add Samuel Bell to that list. And maybe those daughters of his. They're a pair of snakes, both of them." He pressed his lips together and rolled them a couple of times.

I toasted him again, then took a sip. "To outliving our enemies."

He nodded and gulped down the rest of his drink. "With that goal in mind, I need to get some sleep before the actual sun rises."

I nodded and watched as he stood and stepped out of the kitchen.

I finished my tea and put the empty mugs in the sink. Now the adrenaline from the attack had finally subsided, I was exhausted. Hopefully enough to get some sleep myself.

With the house in silence, I slipped up the stairs and into my room.

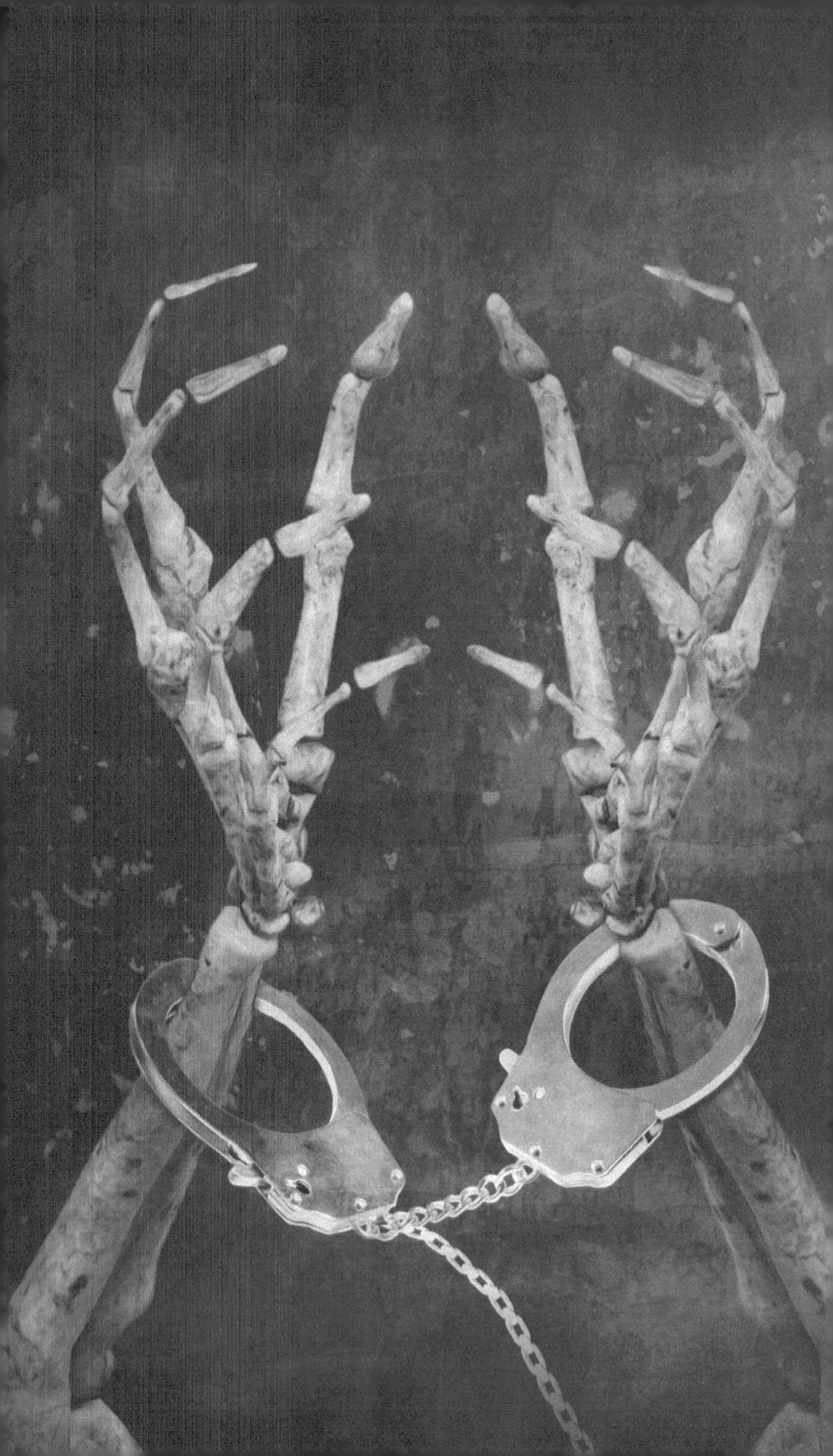

CHAPTER 24

MINA

"I don't like it when people attack me." Reuben's gaze scanned the office.

I stood near the door, Gianni beside me. Damon and the twins were near the window.

"None of us does, boss," Gianni said. He leaned against the corner of Reuben's desk, his palm on the dark wood.

"None of us like being attacked, or none of us like it when Reuben is?" Hunter asked. "Just for clarification."

"Both," Gianni said. "I'm sorry I didn't make that clearer for you."

Hunter grinned. "No problem."

Reuben cleared his throat. "I don't like it when people attack any of us."

"There's been no further sightings of Kurt," Damon said. "Not before we saw Frank and not after the attack. To the surprise of no one, Frank has disappeared off the face of the earth. Whatever his real name is, is anyone's guess."

"I'm guessing it's not Gustav," Gianni remarked. "When I said that name, he gave me a blank look. If he was actually Gustav, he would have at least twitched."

"That narrows it down," Damon said sarcastically. "We can rule out a couple of thousand men."

"Does it matter who he was?" Parker asked. "He was probably just a random dude in the wrong place at the wrong time."

"I don't think his resemblance to Kurt was a coincidence," I said softly. "It might be, but they might be related."

"We should check with Daisy Lasalle to see if they have a relative with a resemblance to that prick," Damon said.

Reuben nodded. "Do it."

"I find myself conflicted," Hunter said. "Frank might be his twin. On one hand, twins are cool. On the other, Kurt is an asshole."

"It's possible to be a twin and an asshole at the same time," Damon said pointedly.

Hunter turned to Parker. "I think he's talking about us."

Parker squinted at Damon. "I think so too."

In unison, they flipped Damon off.

He flipped them off in return.

Both twins grinned.

"I don't think Kurt has a twin, but I can speak to

Daze," I offered. I'd welcome the chance to spend more time with her. Even if it meant talking about him.

"All right," Reuben agreed. "You and Gianni go to Dusk Bay and speak to her. She should know about the attack. Kurt clearly has more resources than we previously assumed. But wait a few days. Let things simmer down. We'll give Damon's contacts time to keep looking for him and how he organised the attack. I don't want you going anywhere without me being sure you won't be ambushed."

"I don't want that either," Gianni agreed. "Not that we can't take care of ourselves, but I'd prefer not to be dealing with eight attackers when there's only two of us. Six or seven maybe." He gestured his hands back and forth. "But not eight. Especially not without Damon and his car smashing skills." He jerked a thumb towards the other man.

"You could crash a car if you had to," Damon said. "Knowing you, you'd enjoy it."

"You're so sweet," Gianni told him.

Damon rolled his eyes.

"They should just kiss and get it over with," Hunter whispered loudly.

"Maybe I should shoot you and get it over with?" Damon suggested.

Hunter grinned. "We all know you won't do that. Parker and I are too useful."

"Is that what they call it these days?" Damon asked. "Useful?"

"I think he's insulting us again," Parker said.

"Enough." Reuben's voice was low, but forceful. "In case you've forgotten, we could have been killed last night. Let's focus on the matter at hand. You can insult each other on your own time."

All three of them fell silent. The twins even looked slightly apologetic. Reuben was right, we could have died. Kurt was the enemy here, not each other. There was no animosity in the banter, but it wasn't going to help us find him any faster.

"I'll keep in touch with my contacts," Damon said. "Someone has to have seen something, even if they got paid not to see. We have people looking at the financials of any of his known associates, or anyone who might have come in contact with him in the last few years. If he's paid any of them to pretend they didn't see him, we'll pin them down."

"I don't care who you have to bribe, threaten or kill, I want him found," Reuben said. "That is our priority. That and keeping our interests running. No doubt he'll try to fuck with them in some way, at some point. If he's getting desperate enough to send people after us, there's no telling what shit he might try to pull."

"Consider everyone bribed, threatened or killed," Damon said. "He can only hide from us for so long. At some point, he's going to make a mistake and we'll be right there, ready to pounce."

Reuben scrubbed a hand over his face. "We may have to consider approaching Samuel Bell. If we pool our resources, that should make it easier to find Lasalle."

"That's a good idea," Hunter said surprisingly quickly. "I definitely think the Brantley and Bell families should work together. Don't you Parker?"

"Definitely," Parker said with just as much enthusiasm. "I mean, the two families have been at each other's throats for so long. And for what?" He spread his hands. "No one even knows anymore." He gave an awkward laugh.

Reuben narrowed his eyes at him. "If you're so enthusiastic, you can talk to him."

The twins exchanged a glance.

"He'd probably have us killed on sight," Hunter said.

"That sounds accurate," Parker agreed. "A phone call might be safer."

"I'll consider it," Reuben said. He clearly thought they were up to something, but it wasn't something he was going to get into right now. "You all have jobs to do. Go and do them. Mina, stay here."

I stood aside to let them all out the door before closing it behind them. I caught a glimpse of Gianni grinning before it clicked shut.

Reuben stood and moved around to the other side of the desk, ice blue eyes on me. At first, he said nothing. He was silent for long enough to make me uneasy.

"Is something wrong?" I asked. Apart from all the

other things I already knew were wrong in my life right now.

"No, nothing," he said, his gaze still intense. "I like to understand everyone and everything around me. It helps me to keep things in order. But you... I can't figure you out."

I struggled to remain still and calm. "There's not much to figure out. I'm just Mina DiMarco, sister of a famous rock star, a university professor, and a woman who knows how to dispose of suspicious body parts. You've known me for most of my life."

"And yet, I don't think I know you at all," he said. He shook his head and stepped back. "I think I underestimated you. Of course you know how to use a knife and gun, and stay calm in a crisis. We were all raised with those skills."

"You thought maybe I was going to wilt after what I've been through?" I asked.

That was a logical assumption. Alone at night, I did wilt, but I forced myself to keep going when the sun rose. I had to. If only so I could see this through to the end.

"People have gone through less and been thoroughly destroyed," he said. "Gianni has broken people by threatening to torture them. The suggestion of a few horrific methods has them begging for mercy and telling him everything they know. Some people are stronger than that. But you, you're stronger than any of them."

He slowly raised his hand and touched the back of my head, his fingers tangling in my hair. I didn't move while he lowered his mouth, lightly brushing his lips over mine.

Gradually, he deepened the kiss, his tongue dipping into my mouth, holding my hair in his fist.

Reluctantly, he pulled back and let his hand slip from my hair.

"You're mine," he whispered. "One day, I will show you how much."

"One day I'll be ready," I whispered back.

"Don't take too long," he said. "I want you." His eyes were dark, his expression heated. At the same time, fully in control. Contained. He wanted me, but he needed me to be ready to give myself fully. I needed the same thing.

I would have liked to be able to assure him I wouldn't, but I had no guarantees. No timeline.

I took both of his hands in mine and laced our fingers together.

"I'm yours." That was the only promise I could make right now.

―――――

The whole house was silent and in darkness.

I slipped past everyone's bedrooms and down the stairs. At the bottom, I took a moment to be sure no one knew I was up. I heard no sound, no indication anyone was awake. Nothing but Gianni's distant snores.

Smiling to myself, I slipped over to press the buttons on the keypad which would turn off the alarm system for a short time. I'd be back before it re-engaged.

I eased the door open and slipped out into the predawn gloom. It wasn't far, just a five or ten metre brisk walk.

My mind turned over and over with each step. There was no guarantee everything was still in place. Someone might have found or destroyed everything at some point in the last five years.

To my relief, the small house was still present, empty as far as I could tell. Just the way I left it.

I slipped around the back and counted the bricks just above ground level.

"Five. Six. Seven. Eight." I crouched down and eased the eighth brick out of its slot. I slid my hand inside and felt around. My fingers connected with cold metal. I grabbed onto it and pulled out a long, wide box. I placed it on the ground and opened it.

Smiled.

Everything was still here.

I pulled out the phone and connected it to the portable charger I borrowed from Gianni. It took several minutes for the phone to charge enough to turn on.

I pressed in my passcode to enter the home screen. It

took a few moments longer to remember my bank password, but I entered that to check my funds.

"Nice," I whispered. Interest had accrued over the last five years.

I closed the bank app and opened another to reach out to my contacts. It would take time to hear back from them.

I opened a third app, and followed a series of prompts and passwords to reach the area I wanted.

The screened read, 'Sparrow,' in red.

Underneath that, I changed 'inactive' to 'active.'

'Sparrow' turned to green. A few minutes later, job offers started to pop up on the screen. Some I'd accept, others not. The first job was finding Kurt and ending him.

Then I'd get back to work doing what I was good at.

The Sparrow, one of the most efficient and deadliest assassins in the world, was reactivated.

I slipped everything but the phone back into the box and back under the house. Carefully, I put the brick back in place and stood.

I needed to get home before my family woke.

Thank you for reading! The story continues in Ruined. If you've like to read about how Mina dispatched the attacker in the darkness, you can read that in the bonus scene here

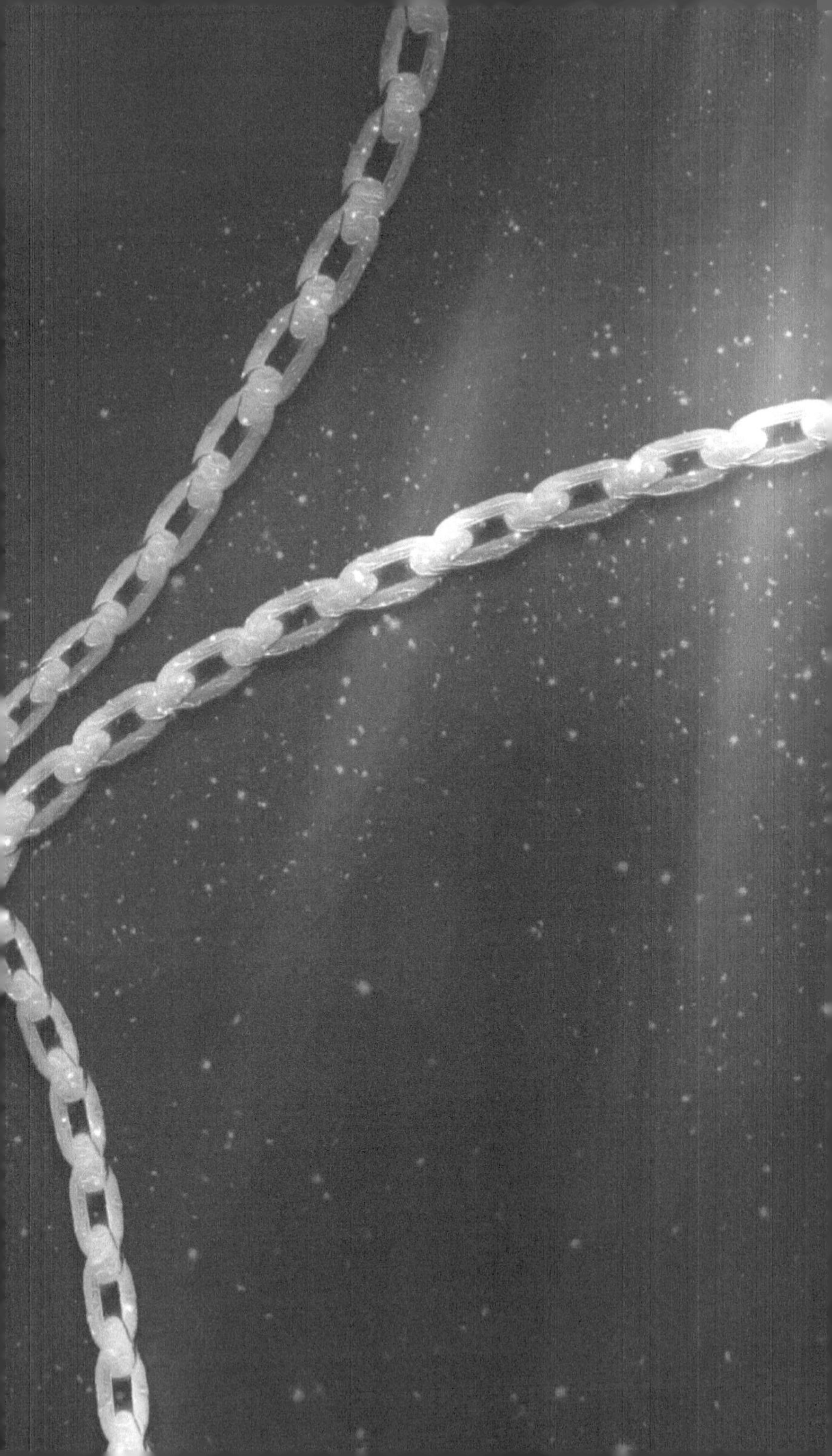

ABOUT THE AUTHOR

Maggie Alabaster writes reverse harem romance.

She lives in NSW, Australia with one spouse, two daughters, one dog, and countless birds.

Jo Bradley writes contemporary romance.

Sign up for Maggie's newsletter! Sign Up!
Join Maggie's reader group! Join here!
Follow Maggie on Bookbub! Click here to follow me!
Check out Maggie's website- www.maggiealabaster.com

Sign up for Jo's newsletter

ALSO BY MAGGIE ALABASTER

Sparrow and the Mafia Kings

Possessive

Ruined

Corrupted

Pucking Dark Hearts

Pucking Hearts Collide

Pucking Forbidden Hearts

Pucking Hardened Hearts

Dusk Bay Demons

Puck Drop

Breakaway

Power Play

Brutal Academy

Book 1 Heartless

Book 2 Cruel

Book 3 Vengeful

Court of Blood and Binding

Book 1 Song of Scent and Magic

Book 2 Crown of Mist and Heat

Book 3 Sword of Balm and Shadow

Book 4 Whisper of Frost and Flame

Dark Masque

Book 1 Bait

Book 2 Prey

Book 3 Trap

Saving Abbie

Book 1 Pitch

Book 2 Pound

Book 3 Session

Book 4 Muse

Book 5 Rhythm

Book 6 Encore

Novella Venomous

Saving Abbie books 1-4

Saving Abbie books 4-6 + Venomous

Ruthless Claws

Book 1 Ivory

Book 2 Crimson

Book 3 Elodie

Harmony's Magic

Book 1 Summoned by Fire

Book 2 Summoned by Fate

Book 3 Summoned by Desire

Shifter's Vault

Book 1 Discarded

Book 2 Deceived

Book 3 Disgraced

My Alien Mates

Book 1 Star Warriors

Book 2 Star Defenders

Book 3 Star Protectors

Academy of Modern Magic

Book 1 Digital Magic

Book 2 Virtual Magic

Book 3 Logical Magic

Complete Collection

Summer's Harem

Book 1: Shimmer

Book 2: Glimmer

Book 3: Flicker

Complete collection

Short reads

Taken by the Snowmen

Jingle All the Way

Also by Maggie Alabaster and Erin Yoshikawa

Caught by the Tide

Book 1–Pursued by Shadows

Book 2 Pursued by Darkness

Book 3 Pursued by Monsters